MURDER AFOOT

DOG DETECTIVE - A BULLDOG ON THE CASE MYSTERY

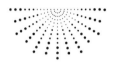

ROSIE SAMS

DOG DETECTIVE - A BULLDOG ON
THE CASE

So many of my readers enjoyed meeting Lola Ramsay and Sassy, the Lilac Frenchie, that I knew we had to write more books with these wonderful characters.

If you missed them you can find the two books with Lola and the introduction to Sassy in my 20 book box set - The Bakers and Bulldogs Collection.

Sassy is modeled on Lila, my Lilac French Bulldog. Lila had been returned to her breeder as she was unwanted. At the time, I was looking for an older, small, short-haired dog to rescue. Something I could cuddle, that would keep me company while I was writing. When I met Lila I fell in love with her and that as they say, was that.

Can you believe that anyone would not want her? She is the sweetest little bundle of love you could ever meet. Well, someone's loss was my gain.

Lila is a joy to live with, though she does like to pinch my socks. Nothing makes her happier than getting out of bed and stealing my socks. It has become such a joke that I put a pair on the bed just for this.

Now, all I needed was a new name and so I asked you, my wonderful readers, to come up with a name. There were some great ideas but the one that suited the character the most was Sassy Pants by Sandra H. Thank you, Sandra, we love the name.

I'm so pleased that my wonderful cover designer has managed to bring photos of Lila/Sassy to life for the covers. Much of what Sassy does comes from Lila; you will have to decide if I can hear her talking. I hate to admit it, but I talk to her constantly.

Read on for my next book, where Sassy and Lola are staying in a sleepy British village with a friend. I hope you enjoy it.

Join my newsletter at SweetBookHub.com to grab a FREE copy of Smudge and the Stolen Puppies FREE here

OH OH

*T*hings seemed so perfect, if only they could stay that way.

Letting out a big breath, Lola Ramsay glanced over the countryside. The view before her was a picture postcard of rural Britain. It was glorious and once more she was grateful for making the decision to come to England. At first, she had been unsure. It was a big gamble. Would she like it? What would she do? Would her nightmares and panic attacks subside?

"Not scary," Sassy, the lilac French Bulldog said in her mind.

"What's not scary?" Lola felt her pulse kick up in anticipation.

Before Sassy could answer the boom of a fighter jet broke the peace. Lola felt her nerves strum like a fine bow but nothing more. Sassy was leaning against her leg, offering her body as comfort. At one time the sound would have had Lola diving for cover but each day, each week her PTSD was receding. Just like the memories of her time in Afghanistan, it was becoming part of the past. She was beginning to realize that the world around her was safe.

What would people think if they found out she could hear animals talking? And that she answered back!

Above them, were 9 red and white jets, flying in a V formation. It was a beautiful sight and one of the benefits of living near Lincoln, close to the base of the famous Red Arrows, the Royal Airforce's aerobatic team. The hawk jets flew over, banked right, and performed a perfect circle in the sky; red, white, and blue smoke formed a flawless O, and then they were gone. The smoke distorted and dissipated floating away on the wind.

"Pretty," Sassy said. "Makes me want to jump up and grab it." The little stubby dog did a jump biting at nothing. Her coat was a mix of grey and brown but it seemed to gleam in the sunlight and looked like a pale lilac.

Lola chuckled. "I think you would need to jump a little higher."

"Next time I be ready," Sassy said and then turned and continued on their walk.

As they passed the churchyard, Father Jackson was closing the notice board. "Miss Ramsay, how are you this lovely morning?" he asked.

"Good, thank you, Father. Do you mind if I look around?" Lola had been told to visit the churchyard and then follow the path behind it by Alice Beecham. The woman knew so much about the history of the place but she suddenly wondered if she should be here.

"No, of course not, be my guest."

"Thank you, have a nice day." Lola really liked the parish priest. His sermons were uplifting, inspiring even and he always had a friendly smile below his salt and pepper hair and expressive brown eyes.

Just inside the wall of the churchyard and nestled in one corner was an ancient yew tree. Lola wondered how old it was and decided to ask her friend, Alice. Alice was a character and she would know more than just the tree's age, she would know everything about it. Thinking of Alice brought a smile to her face. Lola, with Sassy's help, had recently cleared her of a murder. It wasn't their first murder, and she had expected that the sleepy little village of South-Brooke would be boring!

Bringing her mind back to the present she admired the great hulking tree. It was as wide as it was tall; the branches weeping over the muscular knarled roots. The trunk was split down the middle and looked almost petrified. Lola reached out to touch it just as Sassy gave a big whine and strained on her lead.

Lola turned expecting to see a squirrel; instead, she saw Tony Munch shouting and waving his arms as he ran along the path from the field behind the churchyard toward them. "Tyson, Tyson, here," he called.

Lola took an intake of breath as the big brindle boxer bounded towards them. He had something in his mouth. As he got closer Lola realized what it was and her heart did a somersault.

"Oh, oh," Sassy said and approached Tyson.

The boxer tilted its head to one side. There was a worried look in its big brown eyes. "Didn't mean it," Tyson said in Lola's mind.

As he sat in front of her there was no doubt in Lola's mind, he was holding a foot, a human foot.

Lola felt a spike of adrenaline, it clenched her stomach tight, increased her pulse, and raised the hair on her arms. However, her military training kicked in. Though she hated to admit it, this was not the first time she had seen a severed foot.

"Tyson, sit," she said, projecting the words so that the dog would hear and understand her.

"Found this," Tyson said his voice was deeper than the Frenchie's but there was something about him that made her want to be gentle. He was afraid. Not of Tony, who had only ever been good to the dog.

Like Sassy, Tyson was a rescue and though he hadn't told her much about his previous life it had not been good.

"Well done," Lola said. "Can you give it to me?"

"Don't think you should have that!" Sassy said, shaking her head and looking up at the big dog. There was awe in her eyes and a little bit of worry.

"It's okay, Sassy, we got this." Lola reached into her pocket and pulled out a carrier bag she had placed there earlier. Turning it inside out, she reached over and took the foot from the dog. It was firm, and she could tell that it had not started to decompose. Whoever this belonged to, it was reasonably fresh. Could they still be alive? Could the dog track back to where the person was? Could they save him?

Lola was pretty sure it was a him. The foot was large and broad, though she could not be 100% certain, she would bet it was from a male.

Tony ran up to them panting so hard that he had to bend over and clutch onto his knees. It seemed that the little extra weight he was carrying had made the run quite exerting. His face was red, his normally neat brown hair stuck up as he ran his hands through it. "Silly dog, give me the toy."

"Oh, dear!" Sassy said. "He thinks it's a toy." She laid down on the ground and covered her face with her paws.

"Am I in trouble?" Tyson asked. "Don't send me back to the bad place."

Lola reached out and rubbed the big boxer behind his ears. "You're not in trouble. However, you should go to Tony when he calls you."

"I've heard people say you talk to animals as if they understand you," Tony said, chuckling. "If he does understand. Tell the daft doggy... well, tell him he really must come back when I call." He stood up now, his face still red and he was panting heavily.

"Where did you find this?" Lola asked.

"Oh, it was in the corner of the churchyard somewhere. I'm not exactly sure. Is it one you lost?"

Lola gulped. Did he really think this was a toy? With the foot half in and half out of the carrier she turned it over and that was when she spotted the tattoo of a scythe. Sassy had been right with her exclamation of oh oh. This could be big trouble! This could be more trouble than any of them wanted. How she hoped the owner of the foot was still alive.

"Tony, I hate to say this, but this is not a toy. This is a real foot and if I'm not mistaken, it belongs to Alexander Petrov."

Lola saw Tony pale visibly. The Russian was well-known in these parts and so was his family. This could be very bad news. Tony rubbed his hands down his jeans, it was an instinctive gesture for she was sure he hadn't touched the foot.

"Oh, crap," Tony said and his face colored as he looked behind them. "Sorry, Father."

Lola had not seen the parish priest come over to them, he must have been drawn by the shouting.

"Not a problem. Did I hear you say there was a foot? What do you mean?"

Lola turned and showed the vicar the foot. She knew that time was of the essence here. If Alexander was still alive, the sooner they found him the better. "Can you call an ambulance and the police?" Lola asked.

Father Jackson nodded. "Of course."

"And place this in some ice, just in case." Lola doubted that the foot was in a good enough condition to be reattached, it was cold which did not bode well for its owner, but it was better to be on the safe side.

"Yes, I will go now." Father Jackson reached out gingerly to take the package.

"Tony, Tony," Lola called a little sharper to drag Tony's eyes away from the bag containing the foot.

"Yes, sorry." He was absent-mindedly rubbing the boxer behind the ears. Tyson was leaning into his hand but still looked a little nervous.

"Show me where you found this, maybe he's still alive."

"Oh, God, oops... sorry, sorry, yeah, it was... oh, somewhere over there." He pointed.

"Show me, I'm hoping the dogs can track back to wherever Alexander is."

"Yes!" Sassy let out an excited yip, she loved nothing more than searching for something. "Come on, Tyson, we're going hunting."

"Okay," Tyson said and trotted along behind them looking a little happier.

As they crossed the churchyard Lola had a real bad feeling about this. Would they find Alexander? If they did, what state would he be in? Would it be too late?

RUSHING FOR THE RUSSIAN

ony zig-zagged across the churchyard heading towards the back wall. "I just can't remember," he said, scratching his head and making his brown hair stand even more on end.

Lola was not used to the normally immaculate-looking man appearing in such a state but she had more on her mind. If Alexander had any chance of surviving then the sooner they found him the better. Somehow, the cold pit in her stomach told her that his survival was doubtful, but she wouldn't give up, not until she was sure either way.

"Maybe the dogs can help?" Lola said.

Tony stopped and turned to face her, his mouth opening, closing, and then dropping open again. "I guess, but how?"

"They can sniff out any sign of blood, or a body," Lola said looking directly at Sassy.

"On it," appeared in Lola's mind and the little Frenchie stopped and raised her nose into the air. Slowly she turned her head taking big sniffs. "Where d'ya find the foot?" Sassy said to Tyson.

"Thought Tony man would find it," Tyson said and backed away a little. He looked around as if he was expecting someone to jump out at him. His shoulders were lowered and his tail low between his legs.

"People have no noses," Sassy said.

Tyson barked a laugh. "You can talk."

Sassy shook her head and squared her shoulders and Tyson backed off. "Only joking," he said. "It was over there, near the wall." The boxer looked to their left and then trotted off. "I'll show you."

Sassy gave Lola a look and then followed after Tyson.

"I think they have something," Lola said.

"Maybe, that was where he was," Tony said. "I wasn't taking a lot of notice; I was on my phone."

Lola nodded and followed the dogs though she was surprised at Tony's answer. Though she didn't know him that well, she regularly saw him helping out in the churchyard and she had never seen him with a phone.

"Got it," Tyson barked and turned to look at them.

Lola rushed over hoping to find Alexander alive but what she saw was a disturbed area of soil. This could not be good!

Sassy squeezed beneath the boxer and began sniffing the soil. "There is man buried here," she said. "Not too deep and not long ago."

Lola rubbed the Frenchie behind the ears and gently moved her away. "Well done, you two," she said and reached into her pocket and tossed each dog a dried fish treat that she kept for just such an occasion.

While they munched away she pulled out her phone and took a few pictures. That done, she gently scraped the soil away. It was cold and slightly damp, there had been a heavy dew this morning. Bit by bit she removed the soil, being careful to not go too deep and risk injury! The hole in her stomach said that this precaution was unnecessary but she carried on with care anyway.

"Should we leave this for the police?" Tony asked. He was absentmindedly rubbing the boxer's head again. The only sign of his worry was how he nibbled at his bottom lip. It was beginning to look sore.

"I know it's a long shot but just in case he's still alive, time could be the deciding factor."

"Oh, yeah, I never thought of that."

Lola turned back to the ground and scraped away more of the soil. It was sticking to her hands and getting up her nails but she kept her head and worked carefully but quickly. With the next scrape, she uncovered an arm just above the elbow. It was cold, too cold. A feeling of despair, of not again, went through her. How many bodies had she seen? How many of her friends had she buried?

For a moment, the blackness threatened to overwhelm her, to drag her back to the agony of survivor's guilt, but she shook it off. The arm was thick, muscled, hairy, it belonged to a man. She worked down the arm toward the wrist. Scraping the soil away even quicker, she dug and worked the soil away until she could find the wrist.

Taking it in her fingers she checked for a pulse. There was nothing.

Letting out a sigh she shook her head and stood up.

"Why are you stopping?" Tony asked and tried to rush towards the body.

Lola reached out and stopped him. "It's too late, this is a crime scene now and it's best we leave it as undisturbed as possible."

The sound of sirens approaching sent a shock of tension through her and Sassy was leaning against her leg. "I'm fine," Lola said.

"Not sure that I am," Tony replied. "I think I might be sick."

Lola could see that his eyes were fixated on the disturbed grave and the white arm showing like porcelain against the loamy black soil. "Go back to the church, don't contaminate this area," Lola said and indicating to the dogs to follow, she guided Tony away from their grisly discovery.

As Tony leaned over the wall, Detective Sergeant Wayne Foster walked into the churchyard. The man was a true Brit but looked like a surfer from California, with his dirty blond hair, deep tan, and broad shoulders. The graphite grey suit sat well on his frame and he gave Lola a warm smile.

"Morning, Lola. We must stop meeting this way."

Lola smiled. Wayne was the boyfriend of the friend she was staying with, Tanya Buchannan.

"I guess the report I got was a crank call, I was in the area so I thought I'd come along."

Before Lola could answer the sound of an ambulance siren cut through their conversation. It was coming fast and would have put on the sirens to negotiate the traffic lights at the top of the hill. Lola waited for the vehicle to pull up and the paramedics to come running over. She raised her hand in a stop sign and shook her head. The two men slowed to a walk.

"So it was a hoax!" Wayne laughed and turned. "I'll see you tonight."

"Wait, Wayne. It was not a hoax, there's just no rush."

"Oh."

Lola pointed behind Wayne to Father Jackson who was walking toward them. "I put the... errr... the item in my fridge," he said. "Should I grab it and give it to the ambulance crew?"

Lola shook her head. "No, you can give it to Wayne. I'm sorry to say that the body is dead. I think it's Alexander Petrov."

"What?!" Wayne shook his head. "Are you sure?"

"No, it's just the tattoo on his foot, I recognized it from the village fete."

"It's him," Sassy whined, "me smells horrid man who went to kick Tyson." Sassy was standing between Lola and Wayne looking rather pleased with herself.

"Show me," Wayne looked resigned and willing to believe her. He had seen Lola deal with crime scenes before and he knew enough to trust her instincts.

Quickly, they weaved their way through the graves and back to the wall where the arm was showing stark white against the dark ground.

"Okay, we need to cordon this area off and I will need to talk to all of you, but for now, go back to the church and wait for me."

"Okay, but I don't know much," Lola said but Wayne was already talking on his phone to the station.

Lola walked back to tell the ambulance crew they wouldn't be needed and then she went to find Tony. He sat on a bench with Tyson sitting next to him. The boxer's big head was bowed and resting on Tony's knee and he was shaking slightly.

"You're okay," Lola said to the dog. "No one's gonna hurt you."

"I hadn't thought about being hurt," Tony said. "It's just so shocking. I feel so silly chasing after Tyson thinking he had run off with someone's toy. What will the police think?"

"They will just ask you a few questions, don't worry about it," Lola said as Father Jackson came back with a tray and three cups of tea and a plate of ginger cookies, biscuits as the British called them.

"I thought we might need this," he said.

Tony took his cup with shaking hands and sipped the strong dark liquid, clinging to the cup as if it was a lifeline.

The sound of a V8 engine driven in anger shattered the peace and quiet of the village. It reverberated off the houses and had them all looking toward the road. A big matt black Range Rover screeched to a halt at the church gates. The door opened and a tall slim-built man ran into the churchyard. "Where is he? Where is my brother?"

Lola had never met Uri Petrov but he was unmistakably Alexander's brother. There was something mean in his features, mean and dangerous. Dark eyes roved the churchyard looking for someone to hit. "Who did this?" he called. "Whoever it was, they will feel my blade, cold and deadly between their shoulders. Who killed my brother?"

Uri ran over to them. He was an impressive man with tattoos curling out of the sleeves of his cream jacket and across his thin hands. Though slighter than Alexander he looked like a man you would not want to meet in a dark alley.

"Were you involved?" he barked at Tony.

Tony visibly shook as he shuffled along the bench to move away from Uri. "I just found him?" Tony said.

Tyson was shaking and yet he still put himself between Tony and the newcomer, but before the boxer could pluck up the courage to bark, Sassy nipped between his legs and bit the Russian's ankle. As Uri jumped back she let out her Frenchie scream. A wild banshee sound of rage and defiance, Uri stepped back even further.

"Keep that mutt away from me or I will stomp on it," Uri said.

Lola remembered. Alexander had made a similar threat to Tyson and Tony had made a threat of his own. *Oh no, this would not look good for Tony.* Lola just hoped that no one would remember him threatening to kill the Russian and chop him up with his ax.

"Where is my brother? Whoever killed him will feel Russian justice."

Lola gulped, if Uri found out about the threat, then Tony could be in big trouble.

THE ERRANT BROTHER

"*J*'m sorry for your loss," Lola said. Even though Alexander hadn't been officially identified she was now sure that the body was his. "Why don't you wait inside the church while the police deal with this?" Lola noticed a white police van with SOCO on the side pulling up outside the churchyard. The Scene Of Crime Officers were here along with some uniformed PCs.

Uri wore an arrogant look, almost a sneer but he was wary of Sassy and kept his distance. "I need to see him." Uri seemed to remember that he should be sad and his face crumpled. "I need to see my poor brother." He mumbled something in Russian and shook his head. "It is terrible, so terrible. My poor father will be beside himself." His anger had been replaced with an air of sadness but it did not seem genuine.

"Crocodile tears," Sassy said and growled at him again.

Lola reached down and stroked the Frenchie. Sassy had learned that expression just a few days ago when Lola was pretending to have emotions to see if the little bulldog could tell the difference. Who would have guessed it would come in useful so soon.

A plain-clothed police officer came over. The man was young, probably in his late 20's, a little chubby with red hair and a pale complexion. There was something superior about his walk. It was almost a swagger.

"What do we have here?" he asked.

"This is Uri Petrov, the victim's brother," Lola said.

"You know my name, how?" Uri asked.

"Your family is quite well known," Father Jackson said. "Please accept my condolences. I have things to attend to, I must go."

"Wait just a moment. I'm Detective Constable Peterson, I ask the questions here and as far as I know, we have not formally identified the body yet."

"Danny Boy," Sassy said in Lola's mind. It was the name that Wayne had given to the fast-tracked, Daniel Peterson. Wayne was not keen on the man, he had come straight from university into the Police Now National Detective Program and didn't seem to care too much for victims. Wayne believed he always took the easiest route, this was the last thing that Lola wanted. If he found out who had been threatening Alexander then two of her friends could be in trouble.

"Then take me to him, I can identify my brother." Uri may have been wary of the Frenchie but Danny did not scare him. Taking a step closer he towered over the younger man, his face a neutral mask but still enough to make Peterson gulp.

"Well, you need to go to the station where you can wait to make an official identification."

"Nyet, I see him now."

"Constables," Peterson called and stepped away as the Russian moved closer. It was like a dance. Peterson took a step back, Uri growled and took one closer. It reminded her of a Paso Doble she had once seen on a ballroom dancing show. The two men's eyes were locked together in a battle of wits.

Two uniformed police officers arrived on the scene. "Escort Mr. Petrov to the station," Peterson said, looking mighty relieved. "He may be related to the victim."

Uri looked as if he would not go and then he shrugged. "I follow you." With that, he walked back to the Range Rover and everyone breathed a sigh of relief.

"You all need to wait here, we will need to take your statements," Peterson said before walking away.

"What do we do now?" Tony asked. "Will it be Wayne who deals with this?"

"I guess we just wait, and it looks like it will be Peterson," Lola said making herself comfortable on the bench. They sat and talked, watching as the officers tented off the area where the body was found. Everyone seemed to know what they were doing and soon a covered body was wheeled into a waiting vehicle. Lola hoped that this would be over soon, she was getting stiff.

"We need to speak to you all at the station," Wayne said, coming over about an hour later. "I can have an officer drive you."

"What about Tyson?" Tony asked.

"Who?"

"I come with, I keep Tony man safe," Tyson said, as he sat next to Tony still leaning against his legs. Sassy was cuddling up to the boxer.

"I keep you safe," she said to Lola.

"My dog," Tony said.

Lola smiled and felt a feeling of warmth as the Frenchie sent her love. She didn't know how she did that. Didn't even know if it was real but it always drove away any stress or nasty feelings and filled her with strength.

"If you wish to come in tomorrow that is fine," Wayne said. "Or, I will be back at the station in an hour if you want to get there for then. There's no rush, we just need to take your statements."

"Tony has smelly feet, real scrummy socks," Lola heard Sassy's voice in her mind. The Frenchie had forgotten the body and the worry as her obsession with socks kicked in. "Can you get me some of his socks?" She was looking up at the boxer, her amber eyes pleading for all she was worth.

Tyson shook his head, his jowls flapping and his eyes darted from side to side. "Not sure I can do that."

Sassy ducked as a piece of white slobber left the boxer's jowls and flew through the air. Lola's eyes followed it as it shot through the air to land on Wayne's shoe.

"Sorry," Tyson said and ducked his head down.

"What do you need from us?" Father Jackson asked.

"It is just a formality," Wayne replied.

"Are his socks delicious?" Sassy asked. "Tony's."

Lola was fighting to keep her face neutral and trying to listen to Wayne, she didn't want to miss anything. "I guess I was wrong to disturb the scene."

"His feet are the best. My favorite part of the day is curling up on them while he watches the noisy box."

"No, that was fine," Wayne said, "I understand why you did it. What we need to do is find out how the body was discovered and why it was by you." Wayne was looking at Tony.

"What do you mean by that?" Tony's face paled and his eyes narrowed.

"Oh, that's the emotion you wanted me to learn," Sassy said, turning her head to Lola. "Gwilt?"

Why would Tony be feeling gwilty... guilty, Lola wondered. Though she was sure the man had done no wrong it still made her curious.

"Can we leave it until tomorrow?" Tony asked. "Do you want us all together? I just feel I could do with a break; this has been pretty... well, I'm not used to seeing things like this. I know I was foolish. I shouldn't have let Tyson mess with the... well, with the body bits... I'm really sorry."

Wayne put his hand on Tony's shoulder. "Don't worry. Tomorrow is fine and if your dog hadn't found the foot, well, we might never have found the body. You did us a favor. It's just for the records, you know what I mean."

"Thanks," Tony said, his color finally returning a little. "How about I see you all tomorrow after lunch?"

They all nodded and Wayne left them to head back to the grave and the gathering of all the evidence.

"Will it really be that simple?" Tony asked. "Won't they suspect us?"

"I don't see any reason why they should," Lola said ignoring the fact that both of the men before her had threatened Alexander. Tony because the Russian had threatened to beat his dog and Father Jackson because

Alexander had been peddling drugs to the children near the churchyard. Still, a man with such morals must have had a lot of enemies.

"Okay, I guess I will go home then. Should I lock the shed first?" Tony asked.

Father Jackson shook his head. "No, you get off, I will lock it and I will see you soon. If you need to talk, call me."

Lola rubbed Tyson's thick neck just behind his ears. "Don't you worry, Tyson, you're a good brave dog."

The boxer gave a happy woof and trotted along after Tony.

"How are your renovations coming along?" Father Jackson asked.

Lola had bought a house with a business property downstairs and living accommodation upstairs. She planned to convert it to give her a place to live and an office for her private investigations business. Renovations had been stopped when a body had been discovered buried in the grounds but could start again now.

"I'm not sure that I can afford to get it started," Lola said. "I've used up most of my savings and though I've had a few good cases, my income is not regular at the moment."

"That is a shame, it will be nice to see the place lived in again. If you need anything you can call me too."

"Thank you, how are you doing... after all of this?"

The priest ran a hand through his salt and pepper hair. "I can't say it wasn't a shock. However, I believe that prayer and time will see me right. I'm ashamed to say that the world is a better place without Alexander Petrov in it."

"I agree, but I would keep that opinion to myself."

Father Jackson smiled. "You are right, however, it would be ludicrous to think that I could have had anything to do with this."

Lola nodded and said her goodbyes, she didn't like to point out that sometimes the ludicrous could be thought of. She knew that Wayne was a good detective, but both Tony and Father Jackson had threatened the victim, that would have to be taken into account, wouldn't it? And why was Peterson here? Who would get the case?

Hopefully, the men's threats would be looked at and dismissed quickly. The last thing this village needed was for two of its upstanding citizens to be accused of murder. Lola tried to shake off the idea but it wouldn't go. She knew they were innocent but that didn't mean that the accusation would leave them unscathed. It was awful how the press could convict a person on the thinnest thread of information, usually without waiting to hear the full story.

Reporting seemed to be more about sensation at any costs nowadays when it should be about the truth, but maybe that was just her opinion!

SUCH A NICE FAMILY

Feeling a little depressed, Lola left the churchyard and continued along the street. South-Brooke was a small village, famous for its ancient Yew hedges and with mostly large and beautiful houses. She had decided to take a look at her own property which was at the top of the hill, closer to the main road that led into the historic city of Lincoln.

Work had only just started back on her property, following the discovery of a body there. However, she thought it would have to stop soon. Pushing that thought to the back of her mind she tried to enjoy the walk. Why were there always so many problems, so much expense?

As they turned onto the bottom of the hill, Sassy began to pull on her lead. The little Frenchie thought they were going to see Tilly Trotter, the owner of the village shop. The two of them had become firm friends and Sassy had her own bed there and was always getting treats. Often her favorite, which was chicken.

As they approached the shop, Lola was going to walk straight past but something changed her mind. It would be nice to see Tilly, and Sassy would certainly enjoy it.

The windows of the shop were full of postcards with local advertisements. There was furniture for sale, logs for people's wood burners, gardeners and cleaners asking for work, and all sorts of items that people no longer wanted. Pushchairs and bicycles seemed to be popular.

Ignoring the advertisements, Lola opened the door, a bell above it tinkling. At one time it would've had her adrenaline spiking. It would raise the hair on her arms and set her heart pounding. Now, not only did she expect it, but her PTSD was getting much better and she had Sassy at her side.

Before they could get through the door Tilly had run from around the counter to them. Though she must be 60, Tilly was sprightly, with short sensible grey hair and shrewd but kind brown eyes behind her round ringed glasses. She scooped Sassy into her arms and cuddled her close to her face. The little Frenchie grunted and groaned with appreciation laying on her back in Tilly's arms for a belly rub.

"It is so good to see you both," Tilly said peering through her small round glasses.

"You too," Lola said flicking back a lock of her long black hair.

"Why don't you come through for a cuppa, it's been a really quiet morning." Tilly didn't wait for an answer, but turned and walked past the counter and through a door into the back of the shop.

Lola glanced around the shop; it was small, with shelves piled high with everything from groceries to children's toys. It was never really busy, and yet it was essential for the village and seemed to do a reasonably good trade. A lot of the farmers stopped in for snacks to eat in their tractors, and most of the village called in at least once a week. Realizing that she was standing there staring at nothing, Lola followed them through to Tilly's private quarters.

The door led into a small but busy kitchen. Jars and bottles lined shelves that went all the way around the top of the room. The walls were painted magnolia, the work surface was made of brown tiles and it looked like Tilly had been making a dessert. For sitting on top of the surface was a large glass dish. It looked a little like tiramisu, but made with raspberries, and with big piped cream on top. Lola felt her stomach grumble.

Tilly was already preparing the tea, and Sassy was sitting in the corner on the pink fluffy bed that Tilly had bought her munching away on a gravy bone. The treats were one of her favorites.

"Yum Yum," Lola heard in her mind. "Not sharing my gravy bone, Tilly might give you one if you ask nicely. I sit and beg, it works."

"How are you doing?" Tilly asked as she placed a teapot and 2 cups on the table. "You look a little... well... the word frazzled comes to mind?"

Lola patted her hair again, it was long, straight, black, and very fine. It had a mind of its own and as she had been standing outside for some time she wondered if it stood on end as much as Tony's had been. Sighing, she sank into a chair at the table. She knew there was no point in offering to help, Tilly loved to look after her. "It's been a difficult morning."

"Let me make you a sandwich, I have some chicken, lettuce and tomatoes, and some nice mayonnaise."

"Chicken!" Sassy was off her bed and sitting next to Tilly in a flash.

"Don't worry, I can spare a little for you," Tilly said passing a morsel down to the Frenchie.

As they drank tea and ate chicken mayonnaise sandwiches, Lola explained what had happened at the church.

"Oh, my, poor dear Tony, is he all right?"

"He was very shocked, he thought it was a toy at first."

Tilly tutted. "Well, I imagine you would. Who would have expected body parts? Are you sure it was Alexander Petrov?"

"Not entirely," Lola said. "But the tattoo was pretty distinctive... and his brother turned up not long after the police."

"That was quick," Tilly said.

"Yes, it was. I didn't think about it at the time but I wonder how he found out there was a body there... and why he thought it was his brother?"

Tilly chuckled. "Well, if it was Stuart, I would know he was listening to the police scanner. I've told him off a few times about it but he's riding around in a big tractor all day, he says he's got nothing better to do."

Lola nodded, that could be it. She had met the young farmer that Tilly was talking about. He seemed a nice young man, always polite, even when he was in the great big green machine that made the country roads feel very small. But why would a Russian businessman be listening to a police scanner? Why indeed!

"What do you know about the Petrovs?" Lola asked. Tilly was her best source of information. She knew everyone and had an old-fashioned sense of justice. There was many a criminal that Tilly had kept her eye on over the years, and if she got enough information, she passed it on to the police.

Tilly wrinkled her nose and pushed her glasses back up her face. They were small, round-rimmed silver framed. Standing, she began to clear the plates from the table and then grabbed a cloth to wipe it. "Before I answer, would you like some of my raspberry tiramisu? I made it this morning, it's based on the Mary Berry recipe but I have added my own little twist."

"It looks delicious, how could I refuse?"

Tilly served up two portions and then added some pouring cream. Lola was sure that her portion was much too big. When she arrived in the UK Lola had been a little underweight so Tilly had made sure that situation was changed very quickly. However, if she carried on eating like this, she soon wouldn't get through the door.

"Now let me think about the Petrovs, they are such a *nice* Family!" Tilly said her voice thick with sarcasm. "There were two brothers if I remember rightly, Alexander was the favorite. Very much like his father; now, what was his name... oh, that's it, Borya. He came to London when the USSR broke up. I'm pretty sure his money was made from running drugs."

Lola took a bite into the tiramisu and she could taste the richness of the cream and the chocolate, the sweet yet tart raspberries, and the soft sponge that tasted of... she couldn't quite put her finger on it.

"It's Irish cream," Tilly said, obviously seeing the confusion on Lola's face.

"This is delicious."

"Thank you, I love to cook, but often, it doesn't seem worth it for just me. Alice was coming over later so I thought I'd cook up something nice."

"Oh, no, I'm sorry, I shouldn't have eaten it." Lola felt awful, the dessert had looked so beautiful, and yet now they had started it, somehow she felt as if it had been destroyed.

Tilly laughed. "Don't be silly, there was way too much for us to eat. Now, where was I? Yes, Borya Petrov. Most would consider him a respected businessman, but it was not always that way."

"You said he first came to London... how did he end up here in Lincoln?"

"Well, his wife was a bit of a history buff and she wanted to see the castle and the cathedral. Possibly the Magna Carta as well."

"What is the Magna Carta?" Lola asked.

"Oh, well, Alice would do a better job of explaining about it than me. There is a copy kept at Lincoln Castle. It was agreed to by King John, in 1215, in June I believe. It put a principle into British law that the King and the Government were not above the law. It's a very important document. The idea at the time was to prevent the king from exploiting his power. It placed limits on royal authority by making the law a power itself above all."

"I guess it's similar to the constitution," Lola said.

"Yes, only it was written in ancient Latin. It's not that pretty a document but many people flock to see it. Well, back to the Petrovs. They fell in love with the city, and so they moved here. As far as I know, Borya has been legitimate for some time. He runs a financial services business."

"I didn't know he had a wife." Lola said.

"He doesn't now, she passed away a few years ago but the family had settled here and they stayed. Of the two boys, Alexander was always the favorite son. He's a shark just like his father, and just like his father, he made his money in the drug trade. Over the last 6 to 8 months, something has changed. Before then, Alexander never got his own hands dirty. I think most of his business was done as county lines trafficking."

"I don't know what you mean by county lines trafficking." Lola said.

"Oh, it's a heinous crime, in my opinion. The county line is a mobile phone that is used to take drug orders. The crime boss uses a number of these *county lines*, to move illegal drugs across actual county lines. In this area, we're talking about from Nottinghamshire to Lincolnshire, from Yorkshire to Lincolnshire, from Lincolnshire to Humberside. What makes it really awful, is that they tend to use children. These poor kids are coerced into gangs and used to transport drugs across police and local authority boundaries."

"And you say this has changed recently?" Lola said, suddenly she no longer felt sorry for Alexander, it seemed he had gotten what he deserved.

"Yes, I know there have been some major crackdowns on county lines dealing in the country. Maybe the police were getting close. It was around, maybe six months ago when Alexander started meeting a few of the local youngsters near the churchyard. That was when Father Jackson got involved. I know he reported Alexander to the police; however, nothing was done. They couldn't make anything stick. I know that the two of them had words. I hate to say this, but I'm relieved he's gone."

"I know what you mean."

"However, I'm not too happy having a murderer around. You never know who they will go after next. Do you think we need to worry?" Tilly twiddled the spoon in her saucer.

TOUGH LOVE

ola was deep in thought. The idea of children being used to transport drugs was not new to her. It happened in her own country. Children had rights and were treated much differently than adults. Rightly so, but it made them so much harder to arrest. The drug lords used this to their advantage, luring the children with money, gifts, and sometimes even affection.

"Do you think we need to worry, about the murderer?" Tilly asked again, nibbling on her lip as she waited for an answer.

Lola looked up and she could see that Tilly was concerned. "No, I'm pretty sure that this would be a targeted attack. Whoever killed Alexander had a reason. It is not just a killer killing for the sake of killing."

"Well, that's a relief. More tea?" Tilly asked.

Lola nodded. This wasn't even her case but still, her mind wanted to solve the mystery. Who had killed the drug dealer and why? "What do you know about the brother?"

"Uri, I don't know him well but he was always second best to Alexander. Not as tall, strong, or as good-looking. Almost like a lesser copy. Alexander always got all the girls, he was very popular."

"Was he courting? Could she be a suspect?"

"Yes, but I don't think so. He was seeing Sarah Jessica-Price. She's an eventer and from a very nice family. I don't know what she saw in him."

"An eventer?"

"Oh, sorry dear. She rides horses in 3-day events. They consist of dressage, cross country, and showjumping. She's very good at it and out of the country for the last couple of weeks at the world championships."

Lola nodded. It seemed she had ruled out one suspect.

"Are you on the case?" Tilly asked.

Lola felt heat hit her cheeks. She wasn't and yet, she couldn't leave it alone. "No, just curious, I guess."

"I know, it's exciting isn't it?" Tilly chuckled and took a sip of her tea. "Now, Uri, he runs an importing business. He has a big warehouse up on Outer Circle Road. I'm not sure how well it does. I know his father was not that impressed with him; as I said, Alexander was the favorite."

Before Lola could ask anything else the shop bell tinkled.

"You wait here, dear, I will deal with this and be right back."

Tilly was gone and Sassy got off the bed and came over. "Bed is so squishy and like a cloud. So soft."

"Does that mean you want one for the bedroom?"

Sassy sat in front of her and tilted her head to one side. "Like our bed better," she said and then ran back and rolled in the soft fluffy bed grunting with sheer joy.

"All done," Tilly said as she came back in. "Look who's here?"

Behind Tilly was Alice with a big smile on her face. Alice and Tilly were so alike and yet so different. Alice was in her 40's, flamboyant in her red and blue shell suit. Her blonde hair was cut short and curly. Despite their differences, the two were good friends and Lola liked them both.

"Hello, again," Lola said for she had seen Alice this morning on her pushbike.

"Good to see you," Alice said. "I just rode past your new place. The work has started again, how is it coming on?"

Sassy sat before Alice and pawed her leg for attention.

"Hello, little one," Alice said and rubbed the Frenchie behind the ears. Sassy groaned and grunted like a mini pig in heaven.

Lola didn't know what to say. Her finances were not as good as she had hoped when she bought the place. It looked like it would take her longer than she wanted to get the flat and office ready for her to move in.

"Is it going all right, dear?" Tilly asked. "No more buried bodies I hope!"

Lola shook her head. Just after she bought the place some men were caught digging up the front of the property, late one night. Sassy had soon been able to smell that there was a body buried there. Luckily, she had solved the case and had her building back. "No, nothing like that... it's just that it's costing me more than I had saved. I might have to stay with Tanya and Wayne longer than I expected."

"Oh, no," Alice said.

"Well, they won't mind," Tilly added. "I know they love having you there."

"Do you get paid for most of your cases?" Alice asked.

The question was understandable as Alice had hired Lola when her brother and then she herself was accused of murder.

"Yes, but I'm still building up my business. The income is not regular enough yet and the renovations are costing a little more than I expected."

"But wait a moment," Tilly said. "When Alice was in trouble I thought you said you had enough money to pay her bail. I imagine that would be more than is needed for your renovations."

Pain hit Lola as if a knife had been plunged into her gut at the mention of her money. Tilly was right, she had a trust fund. A very large and growing trust fund but she didn't touch it. For a moment she was back in the dry arid air of the desert. Called into her Colonel's office. The look on his face sent ice water through her veins. Something was wrong, something was very wrong.

That had been the day she had learned of her parents' death. Learned that they died without her apologizing, while they were still angry and disappointed with her. It had been too much.

It had been just two more months after that day that she had her own incident. The one that caused her head injury and inadvertently allowed her to hear animals talking, or at least to think she did. The one that took the lives of half of her men.

Shaking, she tried to come back to the present. To ignore the envelope that sat in the bottom of her drawer. The one with her parent's writing, the one that she had never opened.

"Oh, that's right. If you have money in savings why don't you use that?" Alice asked.

Lola looked up into her friend's eyes and felt Sassy touch her leg. The Frenchie was a trained service dog and could understand when she needed emotional support.

Reaching down, she stroked Sassy between the ears and tried to answer. The problem was it was not that easy. It felt wrong to use the money for herself. Helping others was different but how could she explain that to her friends?

THE PAST THAT HAUNTS

*W*hy didn't they understand? Why wouldn't they listen? She was not asking for much, not asking for anything but to serve her country.

"You can't do this," Olivia Ramsay said. "You will break your father's heart, you will break mine. I will not allow it."

Why was it so hot, so suffocating? Lola thrashed out; no, she hadn't done that. Something was holding her, trapping her. "I need my freedom," she said and could see the hurt the words inflicted on her mother.

"Freedom, we gave you everything and you want to throw your life away?"

"Livvy, calm down." Noah Ramsay crossed to his wife and put an arm around her. The man towered above her, his black hair touched with grey, her blonde hair highlighted with silver. "We can talk about this, can't we?"

Panic rocked through Lola. Tightening her chest so much that she could barely breathe. Gasping she tried to make them see, to understand, to forgive her.

Her father's blue eyes implored her to listen. His calm hurt was harder to face than her mother's anger. The last thing she wanted was to hurt them but why couldn't they understand?

"You can't do this to us!" her mother said.

"Lola, please don't be so selfish, think of your mother. Surely, this foolish idea is not what you want. People die, people have limbs blown off. Who would make such a choice when they have options? You don't need to do this; we can provide whatever you want." Noah shook his head but the look in his eyes was enough to raise her anger.

Why did she have to get angry? It was because he expected she would always do what he wanted and that was nothing. Both her parents didn't understand why she wanted to make her own way. Why she wanted to contribute. It was stifling.

Biting down on her cheek she tried to contain her anger but the suffocating weight on her body was too much. "It's too late... I have to leave today..." Lola glanced at her watch. "Now!"

"If you walk out that door you are dead to me," Olivia said as tears ran down her face.

Weight pushed down on Lola's chest and she could feel a cool breeze in her face. Her panic rose to a point where she thought her chest would explode and then she heard another voice. "Here, with me, safe, I cuddle."

Lola burst awake, sweat was sticking her hair to her face and she had tossed and turned so much that the covers were wrapped tightly around her, trapping her limbs. There was still a weight on her chest, not as bad as in the dream and the breeze was warm. Lola's eyes burst open to find Sassy lying on her chest. The little dog looked so worried even in the gloom of the pre-dawn light.

"Thank you," Lola said and pulled Sassy to her cuddling her close, soaking up her love as she pushed the memories back into the past where they belonged.

"Was there squirrels chasing you in your dreams?" Sassy asked, a look of awe on her face. "They chase me sometimes. Nip at them, nip at their heels, and bark and they will run."

Lola chuckled. "Yeah, big evil squirrels intent on world domination. Luckily, I had you to chase them away."

"I will stop them, but must sleep now." Sassy curled up with her back to Lola and as she reached out to stroke the dog she felt her bed socks clasped between the Frenchie's paws. Feeling a lot better, Lola relaxed down into the bed and hoped that sleep would come.

As light began to seep through the curtains she thought about the letter. Would she ever open it?

Lola tossed and turned until she heard Tanya and Wayne leave their room and make their way downstairs. It was 6:30 so she may as well get up. Throwing the covers back, she slipped out of the bed and ran a hand through her hair. It was difficult to keep her eyes open and yet she knew she would not sleep. Those same weary eyes were dragged to the chest of drawers; the letter that had disturbed her sleep was hidden in the bottom drawer beneath her clothes. Was hidden the right word? Who was she hiding it from?

"You okay?" Lola heard the words in her mind and glanced at the bed to see Sassy peering out from under the covers. When Lola had climbed out she had thrown the quilts back and it looked like she had thrown it over the top of the Frenchie.

"I'm good. You look cozy under there."

"It nice and warm, me snugly."

"Get some more sleep if you need it."

Sassy closed her eyes and pretended to be snoring making little grunting and groaning sounds. Lola was chuckling as she headed to the en suite to take a shower. Her pajamas were clinging to her, thanks to the sweats that had accompanied her night terrors.

Switching on the shower she took a quick look in the mirror. The face staring back at her was gaunt, with black smudges under both red-rimmed eyes.

Before Lola got ready for the shower she peeked back into the bedroom. She was just in time to see Sassy jumping off the bed, with Lola's bed socks in her mouth. The little Frenchie trotted off with her prize as proud as punch.

Lola was soon showered and ready to make her way downstairs. As she entered the kitchen, Tanya handed her a mug of coffee. Lola took it nodding her thanks, then she opened the back door to allow Sassy out into the garden.

"Sit down, you look awful," Tanya said.

"With friends like that, who needs enemies?" Wayne chuckled, before taking a bite out of his toast and Marmite and then swilling it down with a big gulp of coffee. "I have to go, see you both later." With that, he placed a quick kiss on Tanya's cheek and grabbed his case before leaving.

Sassy was back inside and Lola poured her some breakfast. By the time she returned to the table, Tanya had made her some toast.

"Thank you. If I ever get my place finished, I am going to miss this."

Tanya chuckled. "I just think you're not a morning person."

Her friend could be right. However, Tanya was always so with it. Always immaculate and so organized. Despite her years in the military, at times, Lola felt as if she couldn't organize the proverbial bun fight in a bakery.

"I think you might be right."

Sassy had finished her breakfast and came and sat next to Lola. Staring up at her as if she had never been fed in her life.

"That dog is always starving," Tanya said. "You have anything on today?"

"No, at the moment I'm free. Do you have something in mind?"

Before Tanya could answer Lola's cell phone rang. Shrugging, she answered it. "Lola Ramsey, Private Detective, how may I help you?"

"My name is June Smith, how soon could you help me?"

Well, that was a strange question. "What exactly do you need help with, June?"

"My father has gone missing, he has dementia, I'm really worried."

It looked like she didn't have a free morning after all. "Give me your address, June, and I'll be there straight away."

THE MISSING MAN

*A*s always when she had a new case, Lola felt a sense of excitement. This was something she could do, this was where she could make a difference and she couldn't wait to start.

With Sassy strapped to the seatbelt, she set off to make the drive. It would take about 15 to 20 minutes. She had to drive down to the bypass, along for two junctions, and then turn back into town. The satnav would guide her from there but it didn't sound too difficult to find.

As she drove she went over what June had said. Her father, John Smith had lost his wife of 50 years just two months ago. He had been suffering from dementia at the time, but this shock had made it much worse. He was still fit and loved to walk. Lola was meeting June at her father's house where she had found him missing last night. She had called the police, and waited, hoping he would return.

Lola pulled up outside a neat end terrace house. There was a small but tidy front garden with what she thought was a yucca growing in the middle of it. The grass around it was well mown, and the blue door was clean as were the windows and windowsills.

Unclipping Sassy from her harness, Lola quickly put on the dog's service jacket. It was yellow and had the words "Service Dog" written on it. It allowed them to get in almost everywhere and Lola felt that it gave her customers a sense of reassurance. Lola clicked on her lead. "Are you ready to help me find this man?"

"Always ready, I'm prepared for a good sniffy sniff."

Lola picked her up and got out of the car, putting her down on the pavement as they made their way to the front door.

Before Lola could knock on the door, it was opened by a pretty blonde woman in her mid-30s. She was a little bit plump and wearing jeans and a matching blue T-shirt. Her blonde hair was scraped back into a ponytail and her eyes were red-rimmed, she had obviously been crying. Lola hoped that her own eyes didn't give away her tiredness.

"Come in, come in," June said and ushered her down a short dark hall and into a bright kitchen. The kitchen units were green shaker and they surrounded a small table. "Where do we start?" June asked.

"Well, you told me a lot about your father. Does he drive at all?"

June shook her head. "No, they gave the car up a few years ago. I can't bear to lose him too."

"Don't worry, it is early days and I'm sure he has just wandered off and got a little lost. How long has he lived here?"

"Over 30 years. Is that important?"

Lola could see that the woman was distraught and she wanted to move this on as quickly as she could but still give June as much reassurance as she could. Sassy could track him, but it had already been one night and many people would've walked over the same footpath. The longer they left it, the harder it would be for the little dog to pick up the scent. "If he had only lived here a few years, then the first place I would've tried was his old home. What I want you to do now, is to take this plastic bag." Lola pulled a clean plastic bag out of her pocket and handed it to June.

"Put your hand inside as I have, then I want you to find something that your father will have touched and I want you to place the bag around it without touching the item yourself. Can you do that?"

June nodded. "His pajamas are on the bed, would they do?"

"They will be perfect."

"I will just be a moment."

Lola nodded and smiled at her. When June had left the room Lola looked down at Sassy. "The lady's going to give you something of her father's. I want you to smell it and then look to see if we can find him."

"I think I smelly him already. I find him, no worries."

Lola scratched the Frenchie behind the ears. What would she do without her?

Once June returned, Lola took Sassy outside the house and without touching the pajamas opened up the bag and let the Frenchie have a big sniff. It always amused Lola how Sassy would exaggerate her sniffing when Lola asked her to do it.

Sassy stuck her nose into the bag and sniffed in noisily again and again.

"Have you got it?"

Sassy pulled her head out of the bag looked up at Lola and nodded. "Me got it."

Lola turned to see June watching them. "Stay here, in case he comes back. If he does just let me know, it's no problem. Now, this first bit might take us a while, don't worry about that, it's normal. Once we get moving, you stay here and I will let you know as soon as I find anything."

"I just wish he would come home, I miss him so much. What if something happened to him? What if he is lying hurt somewhere?"

"Don't think like that. Now, we are going to go and see what we can find."

June nodded.

Lola pointed to the tarmac outside the house. "Can you find him?" she asked Sassy.

"This way, already got it while you were gassing," Sassy said and then trotted off down the road to the left of them.

Lola wanted to laugh but she knew it would be inappropriate. Gassing was a word that Sassy had heard Roy Patterdale say at church the previous Sunday. The conversation had gone something like, "the women are always gassing". At first, Sassy had thought that he meant that they were always passing wind and she had started snorting and coughing with laughter. It was only later when they were in private that Lola was able to tell her what it really meant. It looked like it was going to be one of Sassy's favorite words.

Lola was amazed at how fast the Frenchie could track, especially as they were currently on the tarmac path. When the person had just walked past something then the scent would hang in the air. The longer it was since they had traveled that way then the less air scent there would be. However, it seemed like the tarmac was holding the scent well and Sassy was head down and charging, determined to find John.

At the end of the streets, they turned left and walked all the way down that street, before turning right. "Have you still got it?" Lola asked.

"Yes, very strong." Sassy hardly lifted her nose and kept trotting along as fast as her little legs would carry her.

They came to a T junction, Sassy crossed the road and for a moment she lost the scent. She checked left and then right and then left, then the little Frenchie wagged her tail, her head went down and she was storming again. She had it. Lola was excited, if this carried on they would find John in no time.

Lola walked a good 6 feet behind Sassy letting her track-back if she lost the trail without her own scent further confusing the little dog. So far, Sassy had almost always been tracking down the middle of the footpath. Then she stopped and turned to her left towards the road. "Oh-oh," Sassy said and sat down staring across the road.

"What is it?" Lola asked feeling her stomach turning. So far she had been confident and sure of where the trail led.

"Scent just gone," Sassy said. "Can't find." She hung her head a little bit as if she was sorry.

Lola was confused, where could he have gone, and then she noticed the pole next to the curb. A board was attached to it with a bus timetable. Looking up the pole she realized they were at a bus stop. John must've gotten on a bus, but where would he have gone?

THE MAYBE CLUE

*L*ola felt crushed with disappointment. Everything had been going so well and then they ended up at a dead end. What would she tell June?

They made the walk back and as she went past a shop, on the off chance, Lola called in. June had sent a picture of John to her phone and she asked around in the shop. The woman knew him but hadn't seen him recently. Lola left her phone number and she promised that if she saw him she would call.

When she got back to the house the disappointment on June's face was almost too much to bear.

"You didn't find him? What are we going to do?"

Lola made June a cup of tea and sat down and asked her some more questions. It turned out that John had grown up in South-Brooke, moving to his current house when he married. When she got all the information she needed, she rang a friend at the local radio station and sent her a photo of John. As they sat and drank the tea, the radio station made a broadcast about the missing man and told everyone that his photo was on their Facebook page.

"What should I do now?" June asked.

"We have to wait for a sighting of your father. I know this is hard, but do not worry, I am sure he's just lost."

June reached down and Lola realized that Sassy had gone and laid her head on her leg. It was her way of offering comfort and support and it always helped.

"Now, as your father used to live in South-Brooke I'm going to go back there and ask around. I will have my phone on me and if you need me, call me at any time."

June nodded, but it was clear she was trying to hold onto the tears that were threatening to fall. Lola reached out and took her hand. "We will find him."

As she drove back to the village, Lola placed a call to Wayne. Though he didn't work in missing persons, she knew he would help. And he did, he promised to take a walk down and speak to the person who was on the case. It didn't mean they would find him, but it probably meant they would take things a little bit more seriously.

June had told her that her father's family was very engaged with the church so she decided to go and see Father Jackson. She hoped that he would've recovered from the shock of the previous day.

"Good morning," Lola said as she walked into the churchyard to see both Tony and the father walking around to the back of the church with Tyson, the boxer walking along behind. As he heard Lola's voice, the big dog turned and then bounded over to them.

"Tyson, Tyson no!" Tony called.

"It's okay," Lola shouted as the boxer bounded up to Sassy and the two of them said hello. "Steady there, boy," Lola said to Tyson.

"I was just so excited to see you," Tyson said.

"Ah, good morning, Lola. You're just the person we wanted to see," Father Jackson said. "Can you come back here with us please?"

"I hope nothing's wrong," Lola said, feeling a spark of adrenaline as she wondered if they had found another body. Tony looked tired, but there again so did she. Somehow, she didn't imagine they got much sleep last night either.

The father was shaking his head. "We are not sure... well... it's not exactly a crime but something strange is going on."

Lola was intrigued; however, it seemed he wasn't going to tell her anything more and wanted to show her something instead.

Lola was led around the back of the church and behind a row of trees to a shed. It was where Tony and the father kept the tools for maintaining the church grounds. They opened the doors and showed her inside. In the doorway and the center, it looked neat and tidy but the edges were piled high with all sorts of equipment around the sides and the back. There were pieces of wood stacked against the back and all sorts of tools, as well as a mower in the front. Crates and general brick-a-brack filled every bit of space except for a desk, a bookcase, and a chair.

"These are my workbooks," Tony said, pointing to the bookshelf with a row of books. I write down whenever I come and what I do. Sometimes Father Jackson leaves me a list of things he would like me to do. I tick them off when I've done them."

Lola nodded, feeling a little bit confused. "I see."

"Do you?" Tony asked and pointed along the shelf. There was a gap, one of the books was missing.

"Is one of the books missing?" Lola asked wondering why this mattered.

"Exactly," Tony said.

"But it's worse than that," Father Jackson added. "On the top of the shelf, I keep my old Bible. I left it there because sometimes I like to grab one of the chairs," he pointed to the side of the shed where there were some wooden chairs stacked, "and sit in the churchyard and read. Now, who would take a workbook and a Bible?"

"It is very strange," Lola said. "Have there been any kids around recently?"

Father Jackson laughed. "Oh, of course. I caught ½ a dozen of the primary schoolchildren in the churchyard about a week ago. They were hiding and laughing and joking and they didn't know I was listening. They were making bets on who dared go into the church and..." He stopped and chuckled. "Well, who dared go into the church and blow raspberries. You should've seen their faces when they saw me."

Lola and Tony could not help it, they burst out laughing and as they did both Sassy and Tyson seemed to laugh too. The two dogs were grunting and snorting but stopped quickly when Tony looked at them.

"Well, I guess that's one mystery solved. I know this is awful of them to do this but I'm sure they didn't really mean any harm. If you let me know which ones were here, I can see if I can get the book and Bible back for you."

"Don't worry about it," Father Jackson said. "I will see them in a few days and I will make sure that they bring them back. As you said, no real harm was done, but they do need to learn to respect where respect is due."

"I'm pleased that's solved," Lola said. "Now, I wonder, do you remember John Smith?" Lola pulled out her phone and scrolled to the picture she had of him. "He probably hasn't come here for a lot of years, possibly not even since before your time."

"Yes, I remember him," Father Jackson said. "Up until a couple of years ago, he used to come here once every month or so to visit his parent's graves. Is there a problem?"

Lola quickly explained what had happened. "Have you seen him recently?"

"No, I haven't but I will keep my eyes peeled. If you forward me that photo, I will put it on the parish Facebook page. It is quite active, and soon we will have lots of people looking for him."

"That would be really useful, thank you so much."

Lola noticed that Tony was struggling to stand still. He almost looked like a small boy who needed the toilet. "Are you okay, Tony?"

"I was just wondering if you'd heard anything more about the murder?" he asked.

That was when Lola realized she hadn't been into the Police Station to give a statement. "No, I haven't even been to give my statement as I was distracted by this missing person. Did you hear anything when you were there?"

Tony shook his head. "No, but that detective Peterson is now in charge. I don't think he likes me. He made me feel... guilty."

"Well, I'm sure you've got nothing to worry about," Lola said. However, she wondered why Tony would feel guilty. Maybe it was just because he threatened the man. After all, if you threaten somebody and then they end up dead, it could make anyone feel bad. Yes, that had to be it.

INTERROGATION

*L*ola made a quick call to June. Explaining that she had more and more people looking for her father and that she must not lose hope. Next, she decided to go to the police station. She could check in to see if there was any news on John Smith, and if not, she could give her statement. Hopefully, it wouldn't take too long.

Lola was led down a dismal grey-painted corridor to a closed door and shown into an interview room. It wasn't quite what she had expected, but she didn't mind. Wayne had been informed she was there and she was told that detective Peterson was looking for her too.

"Not like him," Sassy said.

"I don't like him either," Lola said as she realized that Sassy was referring to the fact that she didn't like Daniel Peterson. Hopefully, it wouldn't matter. They were just here to make a quick statement and then they could be on their way.

The door opened and Wayne's grinning face appeared. When he saw it was her he entered the room quickly. "Did you manage to find the missing person, John Smith was it?"

Sassy ran up to him and he picked her up and stroked her head as he walked across to Lola.

"No, not yet."

"You are sure it's not a windup?" Wayne asked.

Lola nodded, though she could understand why Wayne would ask. John Smith was the most likely name someone would use if they were making the man's name up. At one time John had been the most popular first name and Smith the most popular last name in the country. However, these days they probably weren't even in the top 10. "His daughter is really worried. The sort of worry you can't fake."

"I'm sorry to hear that. Have you thought about contacting the radio station?"

"Yeah, I've already done that and they put out a broadcast already. I just hope we find him soon and that nothing's happened to him. Does this happen often?"

"Maybe two or three times a year," Wayne said.

"How does it usually end?"

Wayne's face dropped, he lowered his eyes and shook his head. It made Lola feel awful. If this was a regular thing, and it regularly went bad then why wasn't more being done?

"Sorry, I couldn't help myself; it's been one of those days when you just want to punch something or have a laugh. In every case, that I can remember, the person was found unharmed."

"Oh, you!" Lola was about to say more when the door was pushed open and Daniel Peterson came in. He frowned when he saw Wayne.

"This is not your case, Foster, what are you doing here?"

Wayne had his back to Daniel and he grimaced, comically, before turning around. "I was just talking to Miss Ramsey on another matter. Feel free to go ahead now, Daniel."

"If I get any more information, Miss Ramsey, I will let you know." Wayne winked before turning around and leaving the room.

"And what other matter was that?" Peterson barked.

"Danny Boy's got his knickers in a twist," Sassy said before coming to sit between Peterson and Lola.

"What is that creature doing in here?" Danny asked.

"Creature! Can't he tell I'm a dog? Not very bright, this one!" Sassy said and growled at Peterson.

"What's it doing now?"

"Danny... Daniel." Lola corrected herself before she used the full nickname that Wayne used for the man. "Sassy is my service dog. She's here because I suffer from severe PTSD and she is growling at you because you were acting in a way that she considered aggressive. It is all part of her training and as long as you treat me with respect, then she will be fine." Lola patted her knee. "Come here, Sassy."

The little Frenchie trotted over, turned around, and sat next to Lola. Gently, she reached out and stroked her head. She wanted to tell her that she was a good dog, but decided it would be a little too controversial.

Danny pulled out a chair, scraping it across the floor in a most childish manner. Then he slammed his file down on the table before sitting down himself. Lola wanted to chuckle. It seemed he had learned his skills by watching too many TV programs.

"I came in to give my statement," Lola said. "There isn't much more than you already know, but I understand how you need these things to be official. Now, should we begin?"

"I ask the questions," Peterson said.

Sassy growled and Lola fought back a chuckle. "Is this aggression really necessary? After all, I'm just a person who turned up walking her dog."

Danny was not in the least bit abashed but he did try and raise a smile. It was not a good look on him. "Then let's get started; if you can tell me your name, date of birth, and current address."

These were pretty standard questions and Lola didn't have a problem with giving them.

"Tell me exactly what happened?" Peterson continued.

Lola explained about arriving at the churchyard and seeing Tyson, the boxer, charging towards her. At first, she had thought nothing was wrong, the boxer and Sassy loved each other and often played together. The item in his mouth, from a distance, did look like a toy. It was only when Tyson got closer that she realized it was a human foot.

For the next 20 minutes, Lola explained everything that had happened up to the point that Peterson had arrived. He made notes, asking her to slow down at times, and occasionally asking a few questions. It was all pretty standard and she was looking forward to getting out of there.

"Is that all you need from me?" Lola asked.

"Was that the first time that you saw his body?" Peterson asked, staring at her in such an intense manner that she believed he was trying to make her nervous.

Sassy growled a little Lola reached down and rubbed her behind the ears. "It's all right, girl." If she hadn't been so annoyed, Lola would have laughed. Peterson might be frightening to a child he caught shoplifting, but to someone who had faced down the Taliban, his act was laughable. "Yes."

She kept her answers short and to one word so that it couldn't be misquoted for she got the feeling that

Peterson was doing exactly what Wayne said. He was trying to fit the crime to the people he had.

"I heard you had a beef with Alexander Petrov. I heard that you're ex-military, that you can handle yourself in combat. Why don't you tell me what really happened?"

"I already did."

"Did you collude with Tony Munch, did the two of you kill the Russian together? Maybe you're having an affair, maybe you need to tell me what is going on?"

Lola smiled despite the fact that the accusations turned her blood cold. Not because there was any truth or because she was worried for herself, but Tony. He would panic over this and she wondered what he had been through when he gave his own statement.

Still, it would not be a good idea to let Peterson know he had rattled her, so she leaned back in her chair folding her arms across her chest. If she had the time for this she might even find it amusing. However, right now, the best use of her time was looking for John Smith not sitting here playing verbal chess with this useless detective. "I already told you what really happened. You will have to excuse me, but I have a rather urgent missing persons case, and if you have no more pertinent questions then I will be on my way."

"I'm sure I'll have many more questions," Danny said. "However, for now, you may go. Just remember, I will be looking at you." He pointed two fingers at his eyes and then at Lola. "If I find anything that links you to this man you will be back here and you will be held at Her Majesty's pleasure for longer than you like."

"It was nice to talk to you," Lola said before standing up and walking out of the room. As they passed, Sassy barked and nipped at his ankles. The little squeal he made was most satisfying.

NO NEWS

*W*hen Lola came out of the police station she made a quick drive back to the churchyard. The first thing she wanted to do was check in on Tony Munch. If he had been treated by Peterson the same way she had, then that was why he had looked so worried this morning.

It would also give her time to ask Father Jackson if there had been any sightings of John Smith.

They walked into the churchyard to find Tony cutting the grass with a push lawnmower. Tyson was running up and down behind him with a ball in his mouth. The boxer looked to be having such fun, for a moment Lola just wanted to stand and watch.

"Bally!" Sassy shrieked.

"Sit!" She waited for Sassy to sit. The little Frenchie's bottom was polishing the grass but she could not keep still to save her life. Chuckling, Lola unclipped her leash and told her okay. With that, Sassy set off like a bullet from a gun racing towards the boxer, desperate to take the ball from his mouth.

Lola wandered across a little more slowly and waved at Tony. He turned off the mower and took the headphones off his head. "Can I help you, Miss Ramsey?"

"Call me Lola, I've just come from the police station. Danny Boy or detective Daniel Peterson if you prefer was... well, how can I put it? Well, I guess I'd say very unprofessional. He treated me as if I was a suspect and he tried playing hardball with me to scare me into saying something wrong. I just wanted to check if he was as... well, as horrible with you?"

A look of relief came over Tony's face. "He was awful. He harassed me with questions for over two hours and treated me as if I was a criminal. I actually came out of there wondering if I needed a lawyer which is ridiculous when my dog just found the... f... f... foot... well, the body."

"Okay, I want you to understand that you don't need to worry. He has done it to me, he's done it to you, he's probably done it to Father Jackson. Hopefully, he will find a real suspect soon and if they can give us a time of death, then we can at least give them alibis. If you write everything in those workbooks, hopefully, they'll be as good as Alice's diaries."

"Alice! Diaries!" The look of confusion on Tony's face was almost comical.

"Oh, I'm so sorry. One of Alice's diaries from many years ago helped save her brother from a murder charge. If you log a lot of your work, who knows, it could do the same thing. But whatever happens, don't worry, I will make sure that Peterson doesn't harass you too much for this."

"Thank you, that is a big relief. I love Tyson already, but I kind of wish he'd never found that foot."

Lola nodded. "Now, I've just got to see Father Jackson and see if there's any news on my missing person."

"No need," Tony said pulling his phone out of his pocket and already tapping and scrolling across the screen. "I can check the Facebook page from here, the father's not that good with technology." He scrolled a little bit more and then shook his head. "I'm sorry, a few people have said they will keep an eye out, but no one has seen him yet. Give me your number and if I hear anything I will get straight back to you."

Lola thanked him and then wondered what to do. Making a quick call to the radio station she checked if they had had any sightings. Once more the news was negative. She had a choice, she could drive around looking, or she could see if she could find something out about Alexander Petrov's death.

As there was really nothing she could do for John right now she decided to go and see Borya Petrov. Maybe Alexander's father could shed some light on the man's murder.

Though she hated to abandon the search for John, she had to wait for leads. Sometimes, the hardest thing about being a PI was doing nothing. How she hoped that it wouldn't mean this case ended in disaster.

THE LION'S DEN

*L*ola was surprised when Borya Petrov agreed to see her. From the research that Tilly had given her, it didn't take her long to find his office. At first, she had wondered if she should go incognito. However, she couldn't think of any excuse so she decided to be open about it.

With a quick call to his office, she had explained how she had been involved in finding his son's body and how she wished to find out more because of that. She had been invited to come in and speak to Borya personally.

Petrov Financials was housed in a three-story impressive-looking building situated on Birchwood Road, just off the Lincoln bypass. It was an easy journey and one that would give her a little time to think. What was she going to say?

By the time she got there, she had not decided on a strategy and as she parked in the car park full of gleaming and expensive cars, she felt a little as if she was stepping into the lion's den. If this man was really as bad as Tilly thought then what was she doing here? If he decided that she was involved in her son's death, what then, would she walk out of here alive?

Clicking the lead onto Sassy's harness she pushed her fears away. If Danny Boy Peterson wasn't going to investigate this case then she had to. If she didn't, who knows what troubles it could cause. Though she was sure there would never be any evidence against her, or against Tony Munch, it didn't matter. Peterson's ridiculous interview had shaken her and Tony. If the story got out both of their lives could be ruined, and what about Father Jackson? No, there was too much on the line, she had to look into this.

Lola was soon shown into an office on the top floor. Borya Petrov had his back to them as they entered. He was looking out of a floor-to-ceiling window that gave an impressive view of the city.

Dead center in the middle of the window was the cathedral. It drew the eye. The Oolite Lincolnshire Limestone the building was built from seemed to glow golden in the sunlight almost as if the building was smiled on by the heavens.

To the left was the equally impressive castle. In front of these two, was the Ellis Windmill. Alice had told her that it was the only one remaining of three original windmills on the city hill and that it was a working mill, grinding flour when there was sufficient wind.

The window gave a spectacular view.

The dark-suited man looked stark in front of it but not in a way that set her senses racing. She did not feel threatened by this man. Maybe it was the defeated curl to his shoulders, maybe just the air about him.

Borya turned and smiled. "How can I help you, Miss Ramsey?"

He was not what Lola had imagined; in fact, he looked like a distinguished and genteel English businessman in his mid-6os. Steel grey hair topped a tanned face and a body that looked a little lean.

"I'm sorry for your loss," Lola said and without waiting for a reply she continued. "I was there when your son's body was found. Please forgive me, but I do not think that the detective on this case... how can I say this? I do not think he is making the proper inquiries."

She looked around the office. There was a large picture of Borya and his two sons on one wall. Alexander looked proud and strong, Uri did not look happy, it was almost as if he was under a cloud. The picture didn't look that old and yet Borya had lost quite a lot of weight. She wondered if he had a new woman in his life. Maybe he was trying to impress.

Borya smiled and pointed to a chair. "I tend to agree." His eyes flicked to Sassy. "May I?"

Lola nodded and let go of the lead. "Go say hello, Sassy."

"She's beautiful." The word beautiful was said with the first sign of an accent. It looked like he had worked hard to hide his beginnings but occasional words would still let them through. "How does she help you?" He reached up to scratch his head and then as if realizing what he was doing pulled his hand away.

At one time Lola would've hated talking about her past; however, Sassy had helped her get over this. "I was in Afghanistan. I came back with a head injury and with PTSD. Sassy helps me cope with any attacks."

"From your accent, I can tell you are not British," he said.

Lola smiled. "Yours, on the other hand, it is very good."

"I have lived here a lot of years. I always thought it was safe."

Lola noticed that Sassy was sitting very close to Borya, it was almost as if she was giving him comfort. She wanted to ask her little dog what she was sensing? As always, the little Frenchie seemed to read her mind. "He very sad, but he has the dark illness," Sassy said in Lola's mind.

Now it all made sense. The reason for the loss of weight, the tan, that if she looked a little closer she could see was makeup, and the wig he was wearing was quality, but still uncomfortable hence his occasional need to adjust it. Even though she knew that he had been a bad person in the past, she felt a sudden sympathy for him. The chances are he was dying. To lose a son before that must be just soul-destroying.

"Do you know of any enemies that Alexander had?"

This time when he looked at her there was steel in his eyes. "I have made many enemies over the years. None would dare do this. It makes no sense."

Lola understood. From the family's reputation, only a fool would go after the son. "I am not interested in damaging your family's reputation, but I have heard that Alexander was selling drugs. Did he make an enemy... did anyone die from his activities?" Lola held her breath; if he took this the wrong way she could be in trouble. No one knew where she was, no one would know if she went missing.

Sassy whined.

ON THE WRONG SIDE

*B*orya's eyes bored into her, pinning her to the spot, and yet Sassy stayed at his side. Lola wanted to call her a traitor and shout to her to come. If she had to make a run for it she wanted the little dog to be safe and ready to flee in an instant.

The seconds ticked past, her heart rate sped up and she tensed, ready to stand. It appeared she had got herself on the wrong side of the Russian and it could be very dangerous.

Borya smiled a cold empty smile. "I understand. That is a motive I had not considered. However, I have not heard of such an incident."

"I'm sorry for the difficult question." Why hadn't she thought to apologize first, she was slipping!

"It is fine. My boy, like many youngsters, is... was looking to the past to impress me instead of looking to the future. Life changes and what was once acceptable changes with it. I will make inquiries and let you know. Do you have client?"

The missing "a" gave away his accent again and she realized as he got more emotional his old voice came back. Not that you could tell by looking at him. On the surface, he was genteel and controlled. Underneath he was no doubt raging. "No, I'm doing this to help a friend and because I believe Detective Peterson would pin it on anyone, including me, if he could."

"I will see what I can find out and will contact you if I get any information, is this acceptable?"

"Yes," she said. "It would be very helpful. I will keep you as informed as I can."

He passed her a card. "This is my direct number."

Lola stood and took the card and turned to go. A thought came to her. "What about Uri? Would he have any idea who could have done this?" Lola noticed that Borya's lips tightened just a fraction before he caught himself.

"I do not think he would, but feel free to talk to him. Tell him I sent you as it might make him more amenable, might."

"Thank you," Lola said. "I really am sorry for your loss."

He nodded and she noticed that his hand lingered on Sassy's head until the last moment.

Lola arrived at Petrov Importing and Logistics on Outer Circle Road. It was very different from his father's business. The small warehouse was at the farthest end of the rundown estate. Though it was large, the painting and maintenance had seen better days and the cars and trucks parked outside were older and run down.

"Can you see what you can sniff out in here?" Lola asked Sassy.

The little Frenchie was staring out the window at a robin hopping along a dilapidated wooden fence. Some of the boards had fallen off and, if you looked, like they had been kicked through. There was some rather colorful graffiti off to the right. At the bottom of the fence was a collection of what looked like beer bottles and litter. The picture was becoming clear. If this was what Uri had become then he was certainly not in his father's favor.

"What you need?" Sassy asked, her eyebrows were pinched together in confusion. Lola could understand, she didn't really know what she wanted herself.

"I guess I want to know if Uri is lying and if there is any sign of foul play."

Sassy's ears picked up. "Play is all fun, what is foul play? Is it with birds?" Sassy tilted her head to one side as she always did when she was waiting for new information.

Lola chuckled. "Foul play... well, I guess she would say it was unfair or violent acts. Ones that can result in death or injury."

Sassy blew out a big grunt. "That not sound like play, but I got the word. I hunting foul play."

Lola had Sassy attached to her harness and she was wearing her service jacket. Picking her up she stepped out of the car and looked around. This really was a dismal place and a burst of adrenaline raised the hairs on her arms. This man was the son of a Russian drug dealer, should she really be messing with this?

"What do you want?" The voice was deep and gruff and most definitely not friendly.

Lola turned around to see a large man, his dark hair was shaved close to his head and his arms looked like sides of beef. He was wearing dark blue overalls that had seen better days and needed a wash. The scowl on his face was most definitely not friendly.

"Borya Petrov sent me to talk to Uri. I'm looking into Alexander's death and wondered if he had any ideas on who might have killed his brother."

"Okay, follow me," the voice was still deep but there was less threat in it.

Lola followed him into the warehouse; in the background she could hear a fork truck working. In the foreground, there were shelves up to the roof and men were packing items into boxes. There were Stanley knives, and guillotines, as well as lots of cardboard and plastic wrap. She counted five different men, all looked like they could audition for a gangster movie and none of them wanted her here.

"Who do we have here, Ilya?" Uri called from off to the left.

Lola looked towards him and put on her most appealing smile. The Russian did not return the gesture. He swaggered over, his head held high, a sneer on his lips. "You found the body, what are you doing here?"

Sassy growled and stood between her and Uri. "It's all right, girl."

Lola raised her eyes to Uri's. "I spoke to your father, he asked me to look into who could have done this. He thought you might have an idea of who would want to kill your brother."

"I was in Europe, I have a cast-iron alibi, why would I know anything?"

"I didn't mean to insult you. I had no intention of saying you were involved; however, I wondered if you may know if he had any enemies?"

"Alexander pee..., sorry, ladies present." He laughed and winked at his guys. "Alexander annoyed a lot of people. I imagine there were many who wanted him dead. Maybe even some of my dad's old enemies."

This was just what Lola needed. Generalities were not useful but this could be. "Could you be more specific?"

Alexander crossed the few paces between them and leaned down peering into her eyes. "I will find who killed my brother and I will give him justice. Just pray to your God, little girl, that it isn't you."

Lola was holding on tight to Sassy's lead. She could hear the Frenchie growling and feel her tugging. However, it would not be a good idea to let Sassy bite him right now. "I'm sorry to hear that you feel that way, your father spoke highly of you and thought you would be helpful." Lola wondered how far she could push this. Oh, well, as her friend, Tanya often said in for a penny in for a pound. "Perhaps I should go back to see your father?"

Uri raised his hand and Sassy strained to get at him. Lola held on tight to the lead stopping the Frenchie from launching at the Russian. Her own pulse kicked up and she was ready to defend or run. However, there were a lot of men here and she had little to defend herself with. After escaping Afghanistan it seemed strange that this might be where it all ended.

PEANUT COOKIES

For a moment, Uri's arm hovered above her. Then he seemed to crumple and he lowered it to his side. "My father said that?"

Lola nodded.

A look of pride came over his face and he puffed out his chest. "There are a few that I know of. I will give you a list but I do not know how you would find them or how you would prove they did this. In my heart, I know the killer is already back in Russia."

Lola felt her pulse start to lower and she followed Uri to his office where he scribbled down some names that she could hardly read and handed them to her. She guessed that she could hand the list to Danny Boy Peterson, or even to Wayne. For once, she did not think that Tilly could help her. Was this a dead-end or could she find more clues?"

"Thank you for this and I am sorry for your loss," Lola said before turning and walking out with the piece of paper.

When they got back to the car Sassy was looking a little grumpy.

"What is it?" Lola asked her.

"Wanted to save you." Sassy had her eyes on the dashboard and was determined not to look at Lola who she believed had prevented her from doing her job.

Lola reached over and cuddled her close. "I know, just being there, you saved me; however, I wanted to save you too."

Sassy snuggled into Lola's neck planting little kisses. "Lovey love."

Lola was filled with a feeling of love and warmth.

"I smell lots of blood in big building," Sassy said.

"Do you know if it was Alexander's?"

"Lots of chemical smell, lots of different blood, hard to tell. Would need to search whole place and sniffy sniffs everywhere."

"Thank you," Lola said and pulled a gravy bone out of her pocket.

Sassy was smiling once more as she munched on the bone. Where now? Should she be looking into the contacts that Uri had given her? It would be dangerous and would take her places that she didn't want to go. Maybe she could look them up online and see where that led her.

Sitting back in her seat she thought about John Smith and decided to leave Alexander's death for now. So far, she had had no new sightings of the missing man. Where could he be?

She checked the Facebook pages on her phone. There had been a few sightings but Tony Munch had looked into them and found them to be false alarms. June must be going crazy so she decided to go to see her again. Before she did, she wondered if Tilly could help. Realizing that she could really use a drink and that she would prefer to see June with some good news she drove to Tilly's shop.

Sassy was so happy to be there and gave out her banshee scream of a whine as they pulled up.

"Love Moley," Sassy said in Lola's mind.

"Stop saying that."

"Why, she so nice to me." Sassy leaned back against the seat sticking her back legs out in front of her and sticking out her bottom lip. It was her sulking pose and was so cute but Lola daren't laugh at her in case it made her sulk even more.

Lola knew Sassy meant no harm and did not mean the nickname in a derogative manner. How could she, the Frenchie didn't have a bad bone in her body. Tilly had just reminded her of a cartoon mole she had seen on a TV program. It was the way Tilly peered through her circular glasses and wrinkled her nose. "Okay," Lola said for she knew that it would make Sassy happy again and she felt like they needed some good news.

As soon as they entered the shop, before the bell had stopped ringing, Tilly was coming across to them. She scooped Sassy up into her arms and hugged her close.

"Love Moley, lovely love luvs," Sassy said in Lola's mind.

"Come on through, I have the kettle on and some cookies baking in the oven," Tilly said leaving the shop and going into the back room.

As soon as Lola opened the door, the scent of peanut butter cookies, biscuits, as the British would call them, hit her. It was heavenly. Sassy was sniffing the air and looking longingly at Tilly.

Tilly checked her watch and grabbed some oven gloves before pulling a tray of delicious-looking treats out of the oven. She placed it on the surface before putting two more trays back into the oven.

Lola heard her stomach rumble and Tilly gave out a laugh. "You always seem to be hungry."

Sassy was jumping up and down on the spot. "Me hungry too!"

"I'm sorry," Lola said. "It's not that I come here just for a free feed." She chuckled. "I've just been so busy. I still haven't found John Smith and I have no news for his daughter. I'm starting to get really worried."

"I put a call out to everyone I know," Tilly said, "but I've heard nothing back yet. All we can do is keep looking and wait and hope and pray that he returns home safely." Tilly took a pallet knife and slid it under all of the cookies. They looked delicious and Lola licked her lips without realizing it.

Tilly chuckled. "I will make you a sandwich and I would offer you one of these but they are actually peanut and oat dog biscuits. Still, the ingredients are all human ingredients, with dog-safe peanut butter so I don't suppose they would hurt you."

"Dog-safe?"

"Oh, yes, there is an ingredient, Xylitol, that is deadly to dogs, you have to be so careful nowadays."

Sassy was jumping up and down on the spot and then spinning around. Now she was sitting and waving her front paws in the air. Anything to get Tilly's attention.

"Don't worry, little girl, they are for you; however, they are a little bit warm at the moment." Then she turned and smiled at Lola. "The next two batches might be best for us two."

"You amaze me," Lola said. "You never seem to stop and you get so much done." For a moment, Tilly looked a little sad. Lola remembered that she had lost her husband and that she had no children. "I'm sorry, I didn't mean to... well, to upset you."

"You didn't, I like to keep busy. Life has been pretty good to me and I really enjoy your visits. Now, why don't you check the Facebook pages once more and I'll make that sandwich."

"If you're sure."

Tilly nodded and so Lola pulled out her phone and checked again. There had been another sighting but when the lady had gone to speak to the man it was not John. What should she do? The last thing she wanted was for another night to go before she got John home. The weather was not cold, but it was not nice enough to be outside all night. She had to do something and she had to do it quickly. If she didn't, she feared that John may not be found alive.

THIS CAN'T BE HAPPENING

"Where are you going in such a rush?" Wayne Foster asked Daniel Peterson.

"We just got an anonymous tipoff. Apparently, Tony Munch and Father Jackson both threatened Alexander Petrov. An anonymous call says that we need to search Tony's house." He waved a piece of paper over his head. "I just had the warrant come through and the team is ready, so we're on our way now." Peterson chuckled. "I thought there was something a bit off about that guy. A likely story that his dog found the foot. Maybe it did, maybe it found it before he could bury it properly."

"Follow the evidence. I've known Tony for a long while and I doubt very much that he was involved." Wayne clenched his teeth to bite back the words he wanted to say. "He's one of the nicest guys you will find and I don't believe he could have done this." Wayne felt a wave of anger developing inside of him. Somehow, he had to do something, he couldn't warn Tony exactly, but maybe he could do something else. What?!

"I don't need you to tell me how to do my job," Peterson snapped. "I've closed all of my cases and I've closed them fast. Which is more than you can say!"

"An open case is better than a miscarriage of justice," Wayne said having to bite back the sarcastic remark he almost added to the sentence. "Who was this tipoff from? Maybe you should question their motives."

"I guess your school didn't teach you the meaning of anonymous," Peterson said laughing as he turned to walk out.

Wayne watched him climb into a car, a sinking feeling settled in his stomach as that car and three others pulled out in a convoy. They would be at Tony's house in less than five minutes. Should he ring Lola? Part of him wanted to do just that; however, it would be wrong and if Tony was innocent then what would they find? Of course, they would find nothing. So maybe he should let this go. He knew he had to and he knew it hurt to do so.

Even if they found no evidence, which he was sure they wouldn't, Tony's life would be disrupted. Having a full team of forensic officers pawing over your house was not a pretty thing. It was nerve-racking. It was heartbreaking. It was demeaning and offensive to your very core.

Wayne clenched his fists. Even though he wanted to ring Tony, and he wanted to ring Lola, he knew he couldn't. At the end of the day, his first loyalty had to be to the police force and even though Peterson was cutting corners, none of them could have ignored such a tipoff.

As he swallowed the bile that was rising in his throat, he just had to hope that no one found out that he already knew Tony had threatened the victim.

* * *

The convoy of police cars pulled into Tony's drive. Before they could all disembark from their vehicles, Tony had come to the door. He stood in the doorway, his normally sweet face blank, his mouth wide open. "What's going on?" he asked.

Daniel Peterson was the first to arrive in front of Tony with a smirk on his face and the warrant in his hand. He flashed it in front of Tony's eyes before folding it away and taking Tony by the arm. "If you can come on outside, Mr. Munch, there's no need to cause any trouble," Peterson said.

Tyson stood behind Tony. The boxer was scared and also worried. He wanted to save his new friend and yet the stress in the voice of the new man was making him nervous. It made him so nervous that he felt his bladder beginning to weaken. In desperation, he pushed his way past them and into the front garden.

"Control that dog, it attacked me," Peterson shouted.

Tyson cocked his leg against a planter of chrysanthemums and at the same time turned and shook his head. "What was this fool talking about? I didn't attack you, I just needed to get out before I embarrass myself like a young pup."

Tony shook his arm free. "My dog just needed to go, it didn't attack you, it just came past you. Stop being a drama queen." As soon as he had said the words Tony knew he shouldn't have. It was this temper of his that was always getting him into trouble. "I'm sorry, I didn't mean it like that. My dog had just had a really hard life, he can't cope with angry voices. Just let me grab a lead so that I can reassure him and keep him safe."

Tony went to step back into the house only to find his legs kicked out from under him; before he knew it, he was down on the floor. Peterson was on top of him wrestling his arms behind his back and fastening them in handcuffs. "What are you doing?" Tony asked.

"I'm placing you under arrest for refusing to exit the property that I have a properly executed search warrant to enter," Peterson said.

Tony felt his anger rising but as he looked around he looked straight into Tyson's eyes. The dog was growling and trying to pluck up the courage to intervene. "It's okay, boy," Tony said, "you sit and wait, there's no worries, no worries at all."

"You keep this up and you will have quite a few worries," Peterson said. "We'll be carting you off to the station pretty soon."

Tony breathed in deeply and controlled his temper. "I did nothing wrong. I just wanted to get a dog lead to keep my dog safe. You didn't tell me I couldn't go back into my own house. Why did you attack me?"

"I did no such thing. PC Gibbons, put this man in the car and get him back to the station."

"What about Tyson?" Tony asked.

"I don't care about your dog, all I care about is arresting a murder suspect and keeping my team safe." With that, Peterson turned and entered the house.

Tony wanted to fight, he wanted to struggle, but what could he do? All that mattered was that Tyson was safe. If the dog thought there was a big enough threat he might attack, or he might run away. Either way, Tony couldn't take it. He had already fallen in love with the big soft boxer, and no way did he want to lose him.

"Come along, sir," PC Gibbons said, "let's get you in the car."

"Can you do something about my dog?" Tony asked. "I swear, I was just going to go get a lead. If you release my hands I can take my belt off and we can take him to a friend's house... please."

"I don't know, Detective Peterson can be a bit of a stickler."

Tyson came over, his head was bowed, his tail between his legs and as he got to Tony he whined pitifully.

"It's okay, boy, it's going to be okay."

PC Gibbons helped Tony into the car and closed the door.

Tyson whined, why were they doing this to the Tony man? What could he do? If they took the Tony man away where should he go?

A NEW HOPE

*D*espite her worry, Lola had managed to finish off a chicken sandwich and two of the human recipe peanut butter biscuits. They were delicious.

Sassy had no problem eating a little bit of chicken and two pieces of one of the dog peanut butter biscuits. Her little lilac tail was wagging so much that you could almost imagine that it would lift her up into the air and float her around the room.

"You do treat us so well," Lola said.

All the time she had been eating she was trying to decide where next to look for John. She had gotten nowhere and for a moment she felt like a failure. After all, she was very new at this, maybe she should have called in a more seasoned private investigator?

"Don't go looking all defeated," Tilly said. "You have done everything you can and more than many would. Life is hard at times, and not everything works out the way we want it to."

"I know, I just really thought that Sassy could find him."

Sassy came up and put her nose on Lola's leg. "I tried."

Lola stroked her head. "I know you did little sweetie. You tried so hard."

Lola's phone rang startling all of them. Tilly laughed, as Lola answered it.

"Lola Ramsey, Private Investigator."

This was exactly what she needed to hear, Lola nodded even though she knew the caller could not see her. "Yes, yes," she said. "Where exactly was that?"

Scribbling down an address on a piece of paper she listened to everything she was told. This was exciting. John Smith had been seen walking along the road towards Jerusalem! "That can't be right. Is this a windup?"

"Jerusalem is near Skellingthorpe, not far from here," Tilly said.

Lola apologized to the caller and asked for more information. Then she thanked them profusely and hung up. "Is there really a Jerusalem near here?"

"Yes." Tilly chuckled.

Lola was so glad she had been at Tilly's. She might have dismissed the call as a crank otherwise. "I have to go, he was seen walking into the village towards Skellingthorpe."

"That's not far away, but there is a big woods there, if he gets in that it might take you forever to find him."

"I find him. I sniffy sniffs really well," Sassy said spinning in a circle and jumping up in the air.

"It looks like somebody's eager to start the search," Tilly said as she packed a couple of dog cookies in one bag and human cookies in another and handed them to Lola.

Lola's phone rang again, "Lola Ramsey, Private Investigator, how may I help you?"

"It's Tony, Tony Munch and I'm in trouble; the police have just arrested me. Can you come and help? I need someone to take Tyson."

Lola felt her heart tumble. If she went to help Tony and his dog then John may go missing again. What could she do?

"What is it?" Tilly asked.

"Hold on a moment, Tony," Lola explained to Tilly what she had just heard.

"Give me the phone."

Lola handed her the phone and listened as Tilly quickly said that she would come and meet them and look after Tyson.

"Are you sure you are strong enough?" Lola asked.

"Don't worry, I'll take Alice with me, and then I'll arrange for Patricia Darnell to look into what's happening to Tony. You go, find this man and give his daughter the peace she deserves. Once that's done, we can sort out what's happening with Tony. Don't worry, I'll make sure that Tyson stays safe."

Lola hugged her, pulling back quickly wiping away her tears. Tilly had become such a good friend and someone that she could always depend on. Now all she had to hope was that she could find John Smith before he got somewhere where the trail would go cold again. Every second counted and she had to hurry.

ON THE HUNT

*L*ola parked the car where Tilly had told her, put on Sassy's harness and lead, and got out onto the street. "Do you remember John's smell?" she asked. "I've still got his pajamas so if you need to refresh it we can do that?"

"I got it, I smell it from bag in car," Sassy said. "I smell him from here. It's been about a tea break since he passed. All air scent gone, but little bits of skin still on ground."

"Okay, let's go." Lola loved to hear how the dog tracked. When a person had just passed, the scent was in the air, the wind could blow it a considerable distance from the actual track which could be misleading. Once that air scent was blown away or had dispersed then there would be the scents left from the individual and scents left on the ground that the individual had disturbed.

Sassy started to track. Her nose close to the ground, she was moving at quite a pace. It amused Lola that she used a tea break as a unit of time. Tilly was often saying they would have a tea break, and it was usually about a ½ an hour stop. That timing aligned with what her caller had told her.

Sassy trotted along the street about a hundred yards with her nose down They turned right and continued at a fast pace for about 300 yards, and then they turned left. They followed this road with houses to the left and then she turned left again, and now they were off the road and on a mud track leading down into the woods. This was the place that Tilly had warned her about. Skellingthorpe Big Woods. It was a vast woodland with thick scrub and brush beneath the trees that would be hard to get through if John had wandered off the path.

Sassy didn't slow down as they entered the woodland. The ground beneath their feet was now muddy and Lola slipped once or twice as she tried to keep up with the nimble little dog.

Sassy went down one of the paths and turned right. It was beautiful beneath the trees, the ground dappled with light. The feeling of the wind through the leaves was almost as refreshing as being near the seaside. Lola had once read that trees gave off negative ions. This ancient woodland was full of native British broadleaf trees. It had once been a haunt of Vikings and had survived since that time.

Now, there was an extensive trail of paths in and around the woodland that people used for walking their dogs and general leisure. Lola just hoped that Sassy could find her way and that she could track John down before he got into any more trouble.

The peace of the woods should have relaxed Lola. After all, this was the first good lead she had received and hopefully, they would soon find John. However, all she could think about was Tony. Why had Danny Boy arrested him? It didn't make sense. Though she wanted to go help him she knew she couldn't. For now, the priority was to find the missing man. Although she would not be present for Tony, it was something she could solve later, or at least she hoped she could.

On the end of her lead, Sassy stiffened. Lola saw the trees above them move. A branch sprang as if a weight had been removed from it. This was the last thing she needed. A squirrel had crossed their path ran up the tree and was now bouncing around in the treetops above them.

Sassy had her paws planted foursquare beneath her, her head up, the hackles on her back raised creating a dark grey line down her back, a high-pitched whine escaped her. Lola felt the lead pull in her hand. Was this it? Had they found him?

"What is it, girl?"

"I knew it. I told you. I knew they were up to no good."

Sassy was pulling on the lead and Lola wondered if she should let her go. Would she be able to keep up? Would she be able to follow her if she went into the depths of the woods? Then it dawned on her who was up to no good. "Sassy, who do you mean?"

"The squirrels! Their scent is all over man's scent. They must've brought him here. They up to no good. Let me go, let me go, let me chase them."

Lola had known she needed to stop Sassy's squirrel obsession some time ago but it had seemed harmless. At the moment, it wasn't harmless and it could cost them valuable time. "I don't think the squirrels are involved here," Lola said trying desperately to think of the right way to bring her little pal back to the task at hand.

"Bad squirrels... always bad." Sassy was staring at the treetops.

"Did you smell them near John's house?"

Sassy turned to look at Lola and sat. There was confusion in her eyes and she shook her head. "No."

"Then maybe it wasn't them?" Lola could see that Sassy wasn't convinced. "On this occasion, maybe it wasn't them? Why don't you ignore their scent; for now, perhaps they're trying to lead you astray and pull you away from finding John."

Sassy tilted her head to the side, she was obviously thinking about this deeply. "They would do that. They not trick me. I track man, I find him." With that, she turned around set her nose to the ground and was off again. It was almost as if the squirrels didn't exist.

Lola breathed a sigh of relief. She should've thought about this earlier; there were bound to be squirrels in the woods and maybe if she had planned in advance, she could have stopped this little interruption. Now, she hoped it wouldn't make any difference. So far, every time they had gotten close to finding John he had eluded them. At least the fact that his trail was fresh meant he was still alive, she hoped that he was still in good health too.

Sassy increased her pace and Lola prayed that there wasn't another squirrel. Part of her wanted to slow the dog down but then, if they walked slowly and John walked fast would they ever catch him?

"We get closer, he near now," Sassy said.

Lola wanted to ask how near but the little Frenchie didn't understand time in the same way she did, often it was difficult to understand what she meant. 'A brief nap', 'looking for Portia, the cat in the garden', were two measures of time that were particularly difficult to understand. She also used 'eating my breakfast', which was easier and 'walking to see Moley' which was again understandable. Before Lola could think about it the pace increased even further. She was having to run to keep up.

Lola slipped and caught herself and carried on. The track was a little muddy and as they rounded the corner they came face-to-face with a couple and their young daughter walking a black Labrador. They stepped to the sides of the path and looked a little startled as Lola and Sassy stormed past. Well, you would, wouldn't you! This crazy woman running through the woods with her long black hair flying all over, being dragged by her lilac Frenchie. It must've looked like a strange sight.

"Sorry," Lola called and waved as she passed. "How much further?"

"Scent is hot now, I find soon."

Sassy came to a crossroads in the woods and ground to a halt. Lola almost caught up with her and had to peddle her arms and legs to slow herself down. Four paw drive was much more efficient than two legs and shoes that were not designed for the woods.

For a moment Sassy sniffed the air turning in one direction and then the other. Lola felt her heart tumble. It seemed they had got so close, was she going to lose his trail now?

A NEW BEGINNING

*L*ola waited as patiently as she could while Sassy searched left and right. In the end, she couldn't take it any longer. "What is it?"

"Scent on-air, drifted all over. Lots of other scents here. Family played bally with dog, it mess up sniffys."

Sassy worked methodically backward and forwards across the ground. Lola knew they had not been here long but her heart was pounding and she felt so helpless. The dog could discern things that she couldn't even imagine and in this instance she really was helpless, all she could do was wait and hope that Sassy would pick up the trail again.

"Got it, this way." Sassy turned to the left and was running once more.

Lola followed as a wave of relief washed over her. June's sad face kept flashing into her mind and the thought of having to tell her that she had failed was too much to bear. "Come on, Sassy, you can do this."

"Me knows, me nearly there."

Sassy was running as fast as her little legs could carry her. Lola couldn't understand how she could still discern the scent at such speed but she seemed positive that she was going in the right direction. They turned another corner and there in front of them was a large open space, in the center of it was a pond with various benches all the way around. Across the other side, Lola could see a man, he had a bag with some bread in it and he was throwing it into the pond to feed the ducks.

Sassy pulled her towards John. An excited whine coming from her caused the man to look around. Lola tried to slow her down. The last thing he needed was for them to come galloping over like some crazy person and their dog.

"Found him!" Sassy yipped out in delight.

Lola managed to slow them down. "We don't want to scare him," she whispered.

"Oops, sorry."

"Is it John Smith?" Lola asked as they got closer. The man turned to look at them and he was easily recognizable from the photo that June had given her.

"Yes, I'm John. I came to feed the ducks but I don't think this is my normal pond. Is there any way you could help me find my way home?"

Sassy arrived at his side and John seemed to see her for the first time. Chuckling he reached down and rubbed her beneath the chin. "Well, aren't you a lovely little dog?"

Relief washed over Lola and she almost dropped to her knees. "Of course, we can, your daughter June is anxious to find you. Why don't we get you back to see her."

* * *

As soon as she got back to the car, and had John safely strapped in the passenger seat, Lola called June.

"Oh, please tell me you found him?" June's voice was desperate down the phone.

"Yes, I have him and he is safe. Probably a little bit confused, probably a little bit cold and hungry but we will be back at your place soon. He seems fine."

Sassy was in the back, her harness strapped to the seat-belt to allow John to be in the front. "I did good!" Lola heard in her mind.

"Yes, you did."

"Did you say something, dear?" John asked.

"I was just talking to the dog," Lola said and then found she was blushing furiously. Most people didn't under-stand about her talking to the dog and about Sassy talking back. Well, they wouldn't would they?

"I understand," John said. "I would love to see my daughter, could you take me to her?"

"That's exactly where we're going."

The journey took no time at all. Lola could feel the pride and happiness that Sassy felt. It made her feel good too and even helped her push the thoughts of Tony and his troubles behind her. This case was almost over, and once it was, once John was safely home, then she could concentrate on Tony.

Within minutes she was pulling up outside of John's home to see that June was waiting outside. What was more worrying was that there appeared to be a car from the local radio station. This was the last thing that Lola needed.

As Lola helped John out of the car June came running over and Lola was aware of a camera flashing in the background. Just for a minute, her adrenaline spiked. At one time, flashes of light meant danger. Sassy was still strapped in the back but she could still project her love and Lola felt her mind filled with warmth and happiness.

"Not bad place, you're here with me," Sassy said in Lola's mind.

Lola nodded, the words chased away the last of her fears. She ran a hand across her forehead to wipe off the sweat. This was getting easier, but she wondered if it would ever be gone for good.

June pulled her father into her arms and hugged him close as tears streamed down her face. "Thank you, you must come in, bring the dog too," she whispered to Lola before she took him inside along with the reporter.

The reporter was a smart-looking man, despite his beard, in his early 30s. "This is Martin Drew, from the radio station, he'd like to interview you," June said once they were all in the kitchen and drinking tea with biscuits. Sassy had even been given a huge-looking digestive biscuit that she had run under the table with, smiling in delight. "Payment made in full, well, almost," Sassy said.

"I'm really sorry to do this," Lola said, "but I have a friend who is in a little bit of trouble and I really need to run to help him out."

June pulled Lola into a hug. "I can't thank you enough. I've been wondering about this for some time, and I wanted to let you know. Dad will be safe from now on, I'm going to sell my house and move in with him. He shouldn't be alone anymore."

Lola was pleased to hear that, and as she got to the door, Martin grabbed her left arm. Once more adrenaline coursed through her and she turned, her right arm raised in both defense and attack. He stumbled backward shaking his head and holding his hands up in an apology. "I didn't mean anything, I just wanted to talk to you," he said.

"You'll have to forgive me but I really don't have the time, and, well, let's just say I don't particularly trust the press." With that Lola opened the door and was through it as quick as she could, she looked down to see Sassy trotting along with a pair of men's black socks in her mouth.

A chuckle escaped Lola. "Where did you find them?"

"Basket at the end of the kitchen. I think they were left there for me."

Lola thought about taking the socks back but decided that June would not mind and it was hardly the time. She didn't want to admit that she didn't want to see the reporter again. No, she was leaving because she was in a hurry.

The thought of Tony in trouble was really playing on her mind and her instinct told her that there wasn't a moment to spare.

THE STATION

As she drove, Lola made a quick call to Tilly to see how things were going. To see if there was any news about Tony and to let her know that John was safe. Tilly would contact all those who were looking out for him. After what she heard she put her foot down a little bit harder on the gas, wanting to get to Tilly's as soon as she could.

Even though it was not far, the journey to Tilly seemed to take forever. However, she was soon sitting in Tilly's back room at the small table with Tilly and her solicitor friend, Patricia Darnell.

"What have you found out?" Lola asked.

Patricia was incredibly calm. At just 5 foot four she was a short woman with a slim build; however, she had a presence that made up for her lack of stature. Lola estimated she was around 60, yet her hair was dark brown and pinned neatly on top of her head.

"Tony has not been charged yet; however, they are gathering evidence against him," Patricia said. She was a handsome woman with a slightly angular face and a nose that was a little too large. However, there was something that made you trust her. Maybe it was the way she kept eye contact or the fact that she listened and seemed to take in everything that you said.

"Can we get him out?" Lola asked. "And where is Tyson?"

"Who is Tyson?" Patricia asked.

Tilly poured them all some more tea and offered a tray of the peanut butter cookies. "Tyson is Tony's dog. Don't worry about him, he is with Alice and he seems as happy as pie. I know he might be missing Tony but we tried to tell him that it would all be okay. Let me send you a picture."

Lola breathed a sigh of relief at least that was one thing that would ease Tony's mind. While Tilly pulled out her phone and sent her a picture Lola and Patricia discussed their options.

Once they had made a decision they left for the police station.

Once more Lola was in an interview room at the Lincoln police station. This time she was with Patricia, Tony, and Sassy, as well as Daniel Peterson. The detective looked rather smug as he crossed his arms and placed them on top of the folder in front of him; however, he gave Sassy a wide berth. "Is that dog really necessary in here?"

Lola had been about to speak when she felt Patricia's hand on her arm. "The dog is a legally registered service dog and she has every right to be here. If you're frightened of her, then perhaps we can get a detective who isn't!"

Daniel clamped his jaw tight and a bead of sweat appeared on his forehead. He wiped it away quickly. "I can put up with it but, I just don't think it's very hygienic." Once more he wiped his brow. "I suppose you're going to want to speak to your client alone," he said shaking his head in mockery. "You go ahead, I have a solid case and he is going down for a long time."

Tony groaned. "What will happen to Tyson? Where is he now? Is he safe?"

Peterson slammed his hand down on the table. "Who is Tyson? Is he your accomplice?"

Patricia reached over and picked Peterson's hand up off the table. His eyes widened and it was clear by how his mouth hung open that he wasn't quite sure what to do. Should he let this woman who was a sliver of his size get away with touching him?

Patricia dropped his hand back on top of the folder and then wiped her hands as if she was rubbing something nasty off them. Ignoring Peterson she turned to Tony. "Tyson is safe, he is with Alice and he's being well looked after."

"Oh, I am so pleased, are you sure? He gets so nervous."

Lola had been expecting this and so she pulled out her phone and showed him the picture. Tyson certainly did look happy. He was lying on the sofa next to Alice and eating a gravy bone.

"Thank you, thank you so much," Tony said. "I will pay Alice back whatever she wants if she would just keep my boy safe until I get out of here."

"Alice is happy to do it; now, let's see what we can do to help you," Lola said, and then she nodded to Patricia who had been looking into the case.

Patricia turned her hazel eyes onto Peterson. The strength of that gaze pinned him to his seat and the color seemed to drain from his face. For a moment he seemed to stumble beneath her gaze and then he took a breath looked down at the paper and then back up. There was something mean in his grin, something that reminded her a little bit of the childhood bully.

"Since we last spoke, Miss Darnell, the autopsy has come through. Alexander Petrov was chopped to pieces with a heavy blade. The cuts were clean and given with some force. Looking at your client, I believe he has the strength to do this... now, what does he have to say for himself?"

Tony shook his head. "I didn't, I wouldn't, I didn't like the man but I wouldn't kill him."

"Tony, don't answer unless I tell you to," Patricia said.

"Tony, you can answer whenever you want, it's you who's in trouble here. After all, you were heard threatening to chop Alexander up into little pieces, and funnily enough, that's exactly how Alexander ended up. Do you remember that at least?"

"I..."

Patricia reached out and touched Tony's arm. "My client will not be answering that question. What else do you have?"

Peterson grinned like the Cheshire cat — if the Cheshire cat had been evil and nasty and intent on world domination. "We have your client's ax that has tested positive for blood, but we will get back to that later. Perhaps your client can clear this all up? Where was he on Saturday between 7 and 9 PM?"

Tony's cheeks turned a little red and he looked down at the table.

"Don't answer that, Tony, we need to talk," Patricia said, addressing Tony, and then she turned her piercing gaze back onto Daniel. The man flinched a tiny little bit. "What else do you have before I have some private time with my client?"

"We are still waiting for the blood results so I can leave you alone for now if you wish. Having said that, if he is really innocent then why doesn't he give me an alibi?"

"That will be all Detective Peterson. If you can leave us alone I would like a little time with my client."

The silence hung in the air, but then Peterson got up and pushed back his chair in a most childish way, causing it to scrape across the hard floor. He picked up his folder, leaned over and stared right into Tony's eyes, and then turned and was gone.

"Can we talk?" Lola asked.

Patricia looked up at the camera on the wall and once the red light had turned off she nodded.

"Peterson is right, that is the easiest thing," she said to Tony, "if you can give us an alibi then this will all go away. However, I will need to ask you about the blood on your ax."

Tony's cheeks were most definitely pink. This was not like him at all, what was he worried about?

Sassy was suddenly at his side and rubbing her head along his leg. He reached down and rubbed her head, there was a sad look in his eye. One that almost broke Lola's heart. Something was wrong here, there was something he wasn't telling her she just wished she could work out what it was. Surely, he couldn't have done this?

HIDING SOMETHING

*T*ony let out a long sigh and stroked Sassy once more before scooping her up into his arms and cuddling her close. "People don't realize how much of a comfort pets are. I had forgotten how much I loved my little spaniel, how much I missed him until I got Tyson. My life was empty, I had nothing and that dog has just filled a great big hole."

"Can you tell us where you were Saturday between 7 and 9 PM? Patricia asked.

Tony shook his head and looked a little worried. "I imagine I was at home, if not, I would be at the church-yard. But no one can confirm that, no one can verify where I was or if I was at home."

"Were you at home?" Patricia asked and there was something in the way that she asked the question that made Lola realize that she doubted his answer. "Remember, whatever you say here is between us. It is private, it is confidential, I am not interested in what happened I am just here to represent you in the best way I can."

Tony stood up and put Sassy down on the floor. "I didn't kill him. The ax is easy, I cut my leg about three weeks ago. It was really silly and I bled a lot. I'm sure we can prove it's my blood."

Patricia looked through the file in front of her. "Yeah, I'm pretty sure we can. But we really could do with an alibi?"

"What can I say? I'm a sad old guy who lives alone with his dog. I don't have much of an alibi."

"I understand." Patricia asked a series of other questions while Lola and Sassy sat and listened.

"I know you can't answer me," Sassy said in Lola's mind, "but Tony man stressed when you ask about Saturday. He hiding something. Don't think he's bad though. When asked if he killed that man, he answered truthfully."

Lola leaned down and cuddled up to Sassy. Whispering her gratitude for the little dog's input. Even though, this time it was pretty much the same as her own instincts.

"Okay, are we ready to get Daniel back in?" Patricia asked.

They all nodded and so she left the room to bring him back.

Once he was down, once more looking quite smug and pleased with himself, Patricia began.

"As you said, you found an ax with blood on it," she said.

"Yes, we have and it's just been tested. In fact, we probably have those tests back by now. Why don't we take a look and forget all this innocent nonsense."

"That sounds like a good idea," Patricia said.

Peterson waved his hand at the two-way mirror in front of him and within seconds somebody came in the door and handed him a folder. It was PC Gibbons and his face was as red as the folder he was carrying. He was not happy with the information he was handing over; however, Peterson didn't seem to notice. He took the folder, dropped it on the table with a flourish, and opened it without looking.

Slowly, he lowered his eyes to read the results. "What do we have here?" The smile slipped off his face and his eyes darted down to the page and then up to Patricia. Though her own face was professional and guarded, it was still clear to see that she was pleased.

"Let me save you the trouble," Patricia said. "You will find that the blood is AB negative, a very rare blood type with only 1% of the UK population possessing it. You may not have tested him yet; however, you will find that my client's blood type is AB negative. You may also note that the victim was O positive, the most popular blood group. So, I think you will find that this proves my client did not kill Alexander Petrov. Perhaps you wouldn't mind freeing my client so we can be on our way."

Daniel shook his head, looked at the file, looked back at Tony, and then shook his head again. It was clear that he did not know what to say and that he was desperately trying to find something to save the situation.

"He may not have used his ax to chop up Alexander Petrov, that doesn't mean he didn't do it. Perhaps I can have your alibi. If that is 100% solid then maybe we can clear this up." Peterson smirked.

"My client was home alone at the times mentioned. Perhaps you can check with the neighbors to see if he left that evening. However, considering it was over a week ago I think any testimony they gave would be sketchy. You know very well that my client lives alone. Where were you that evening between seven and nine?"

Fury flashed across Peterson's face, but he managed to hide it quickly. "I'm not the one who was accused of murder, I'm not the one who threatened to chop up the victim."

"No, you're not, however, you have nothing on my client, and so I'm telling you that you need to let him go."

"Just because he didn't use the ax doesn't mean he didn't kill him. Why does he even have an ax?"

"To chop wood for my wood burner," Tony said.

"Don't answer without my say so," Patricia said and then turned her eyes on Daniel, "Well, as you have no evidence, then you have no cause to hold Mr. Munch. Unless you are going to arrest him I suggest you let him go." Patricia's eyes bored into Peterson and he was like a young boy fidgeting under her gaze.

"He may go, for now, however, I will still be looking at this case and I assure you I will find the evidence I need." Peterson pushed back his chair and it scraped across the floor once more. He stood and then leaned over Tony so that they were almost face-to-face. "Trust me, I'm coming for you and I will find the evidence I need."

With that, he picked up the folder and left the room.

"I don't know how to thank you," Tony said. "Is this really over?"

Patricia stood too. "It's over for now and I hope it's over for good. However, I've come across people like Daniel Peterson before. They are the type that likes to fit the evidence to the person. Be careful, he will try to find evidence to prove you did this, no matter how flimsy."

"But I didn't do it," Tony said.

"I know, I can tell. I'm going to run now as I have another meeting. You have my number if you need me."

Lola tried to shake away the feeling that they would be seeing Patricia soon. She tried but it just wouldn't go. Danny had the bit between his teeth and the fool was going to run with it no matter where it led.

TIGER ON THE HEDGE

3 **days later.**

Lola snoozed the alarm and pulled the covers up
tight around her shoulders. This was the first day she
had taken off in over two weeks. After Tony's case, she
had been busy with providing evidence for two divorces,
another missing person who she hadn't managed to find,
and checking up on the background of one of her client's
potential boyfriends.

Except for the missing persons case, none of this was the
type of work that she liked to do and it had been
exhausting.

The missing person, Jonathan Taylor, was a 23-year-old
man who had disappeared two years ago. Lola had

managed to track him to Amsterdam, but she had lost him there and now all she could do was hope that the power of social media would get him to contact his family. It was not ideal, was not the outcome she wanted, but the family at least knew he had been alive and well when he arrived in Amsterdam. She guessed that was something and they had been happy with the outcome.

Lying on her back, she stared up at the ceiling and tried to breathe as calmly as she could. So far, Sassy hadn't stirred. But once the little Frenchie realized she was awake, Lola would be dived on. After that, there was very little chance of her snuggling up and getting a few extra minutes. Lola closed her eyes and enjoyed the luxury of having nothing to get up for.

Currently, Sassy was curled up next to her knees. Pressing against them. It was amazing how much pressure the little dog could exert and Lola found herself very close to the edge of the bed. It was a double bed, plenty big enough and when she got into it at night, she made sure she was at least in the center.

Sassy always curled up in the same place on her right-hand side, close to her knees. Somehow, during the night, the little Frenchie managed to push her closer and closer to the edge of the bed. If it wasn't so cute, if she didn't love having her there so much, it would be quite annoying.

Sassy must've heard her breathing change for she felt a stirring. The Frenchie got up, put her head into a bow, and stretched and then, wagging her whole body, she wandered over to lie on top of Lola's chest. "Time to get up," Sassy said in Lola's mind.

"Go back to sleep for a bit."

Sassy yawned and then laid her head on her paws not 6 inches from Lola's face. "Okay, me sleep here."

Lola chuckled and that was too much for the little Frenchie. She started to jump up and down and pounce on her. Even though she weighed very little, right now she felt like she weighed a ton. Lola scooped her up into her arms and placed her on the opposite side of the bed. Before Sassy could run back and dive on her again, Lola threw back the covers and stepped out of the bed.

Sassy bounced up and down as if she was on a trampoline and then ran around and round in a circle chasing her tail before flopping back down on the bed, her little tongue stuck out of her purple lips, her eyes bright and excited. "What doing today?"

"We have a day off, what would you like to do?"

"Long walk and see Tyson."

That sounded like a good plan. Lola didn't know what Daniel Peterson was doing, however, it all seemed to have blown over. Wayne had not been able to tell her anything over the past few days. Hopefully, Daniel had a new suspect, but it wouldn't hurt to check in on Tony and see how he was doing.

Soon, Lola and Sassy were walking along the street to see Tony. It was Saturday morning, and so she expected he would either be at home or helping out at the churchyard.

It was a beautiful spring morning, the sun was shining and the birds were singing in the treetops. Lola still loved walking around the quaint English village, with the famous Yew hedges. At times they reminded her of green snowbanks, sculptured out of the greenery by the wind. Of course, that was wrong, they were kept this way by a tremendous amount of hard work.

"Tiger!" Sassy said in Lola's mind.

Lola did not think that the Frenchie had sniffed out an errant zoo animal. It simply meant that Mia Simpson's big ginger tom, Tiger, was in the area. "Where is he?" Lola asked, checking briefly that no one was around, the last thing she wanted was the village thinking that she was a madwoman talking to her dog!

Sassy sat down on her haunches and lifted her nose up pointing it to the right. Lola followed her direction and saw Tiger on top of the beautiful yew hedge.

"Morning," Tiger said.

"What you up to?" Sassy asked.

Tiger lay down on the hedge and began to lick his paws. "I've been doing a bit of hunting here and there, a bit of sunning, I might stroll back and wait for Mia before too long."

"Thank you for delaying your morning walk," Lola said to him. Mia was a lovely little girl but she hated to be without her cat. Some of Lola's earliest cases were hunting down Tiger when he had wandered off for his walks before Mia went to school. Luckily, they had come to an agreement which reminded Lola. Reaching into her pocket she pulled out three of the little dried fish treats she kept in there. She handed two of them to Tiger.

"Much obliged, it's good to see a human that keeps their word."

Sassy was jumping up and down on the spot. "Me, me, me, me!"

Lola chuckled and handed the third fish to her faithful friend.

"Be seeing you," Tiger said before picking up the last of the fish and walking away down the hedge.

"Being a cat must be so exciting," Sassy said.

"I don't know, it seems a little lonely to me."

Sassy was strutting on ahead but Lola could see that she was thinking over this, that she couldn't quite decide which was more exciting, wandering around all alone chasing birds or being curled up in a warm bed and hunting down errant socks.

Sassy didn't think that Lola knew that she had a stash of such socks. The bedroom she was staying in had a small walk-in wardrobe, almost a closet. Sassy had been hiding socks at the back of it for some time.

Lola didn't quite understand what the Frenchie got out of them. Sure, some socks must be full of scent, however, the Frenchie didn't seem to mind whether they were clean or unwashed. She just seemed to have to have a pair from everyone she met.

They walked around the corner, going slowly down the hill and Lola saw Roy Patterdale up ahead. The 80-year-old was sprightly and always busy and was currently clipping away at one of his hedges. However, as Lola got closer she noticed that his actions with the clippers were harsh and his face was drawn into an angry scowl.

"Morning, Roy, the hedge looks beautiful," Lola said hoping that the complement to his pride and joy would bring a smile to his face.

"Yes, you would think people would think that, wouldn't you." Roy was scowling even more now and did not turn to speak to her which was very strange indeed.

"Something wrong?" Lola asked and she noticed that Sassy had gone up and pawed at Roy's leg.

Absently, he reached down and stroked the dog giving one more angry cut at the hedge. The funny thing was that Lola often saw him trimming it, however, it had soon become apparent that he was taking off only the tiniest amount of growth to keep the hedge thick and perfect.

With a sigh, Roy turned to face her. "Did you know that these hedges were planted in 1880, that they featured in the Doomsday Book?"

Lola nodded, both Roy and Alice had told her all about the hedges in the past. They were famous throughout Lincolnshire and possibly throughout the world.

"Can you believe that someone complained about them?" Roy was shaking his head and waving the clippers. Lola had to lean back to avoid having her nose trimmed.

Sassy chuckled and jumped up as if to catch the clippers.

"Complained?" Lola asked.

"I can see a murder being committed if this doesn't stop," Roy said waving the clippers to emphasize his point.

MURDERING THE HEDGES

"*M*urder?" Lola said tuning into the conversation, What was he talking about? "If what doesn't stop?"

"Yes, I will murder whoever makes me cut these beautiful hedges!" Roy waved his clippers once more and Lola had to step back and duck. They really were a most lethal weapon.

"Roy, can you tell me what is going on?"

"Sorry, I may have to get you to look into this," Roy said. "Apparently, in one or two places, two large people can't walk on the path side by side together! Can you believe that they want me to cut this hedge back almost to the wall because of that? I know, I know, people come before hedges... but if I do that it will leave just bare branches. Skeletal waving arms instead of this magnificent perfection. It will be generations before they green over again, if ever... I will have to look at those brown horrible holes for the rest of my days." Roy stopped and looked down as if a little ashamed. "It's only a few feet, is it too much to ask that people walk single file for a few feet?"

Lola was sure that she had caught the glint of tears in his eyes before he looked away. She could understand him, the village was quiet, but if every now and then you had to walk behind your friend rather than next to them what did it matter to protect such a treasure as these wonderful hedges?

"I don't know what to say, Roy," Lola said. "It would be such a shame if you had to cut them and I really can't see any need."

"Maybe I'm overreacting, just because somebody complained... but you know how it is. If the Council gets involved, they can't see past anything other than rules. If the rule says that the path has to be this wide," he indicated with the clippers and his arms getting dangerously close to Lola's nose once more, "then they will force me to cut them. I've been attending to these hedges all my life and it will break my heart."

"I'm really sorry and if there is anything I can do just let me know."

Sassy was rubbing against Roy's leg. Once more he reached down to stroke her. "I'm sure it will come to nothing, no fool would slaughter these hedges now, would they?"

Lola agreed and Roy said his goodbyes and returned to his trimming, however, he seemed to have lost some of his anger and for that at least Lola could be grateful.

Lola and Sassy continued their walk and before many minutes they were walking up Tony's drive towards his house. The curtains were drawn together, which Lola found surprising. She wondered if perhaps Tony had overslept. No, that didn't seem possible.

Rapping on the door, she waited for a reply.

"Go away, I have nothing to say," Tony's voice came from inside.

"Tony, it's Lola, are you okay?"

The curtains moved and Tyson put his head through them and stared out the window. The big boxer barked with joy, spattering the glass with an impressive display of dog art. His head disappeared and soon he was barking at the door.

Lola tried to understand what he was saying but it was difficult. The dog was both excited to see them and grateful that they were there because the Tony man was sad and hurt and he didn't know how to make him feel better.

Sassy told Tyson to open the door, she would cheer Tony up.

Before the dogs could say anymore, Tony opened the door a crack and peered out. His normally neat and old-fashioned haircut had been replaced by an impressive bed hairstyle that would make Boris Johnson proud. His eyes looked red and his face was pale.

"Is there anyone else with you?" Tony asked. "Check, I don't want them getting in."

Lola glanced over her shoulder but she couldn't see anyone there. "It's just us, Tony, what's wrong?"

"Come in quickly." Tony opened the door and almost yanked Lola inside. Sassy trotted in and then he slammed the door behind them. Leaning against it as if he was keeping out the devil himself.

"The news is out," Tony said, turning and walking toward the kitchen. Once there, he put the kettle on and slumped down at the kitchen table.

"The news?" Lola asked, however, the dread in her stomach was because she thought she knew what he meant.

Tony turned over the paper on the table and showed her the headline.

Local Munch
Murder Suspect in Ax Murder Case

Lola stared at the headline and couldn't believe it. For a moment she thought of Roger, a man she had dated once or twice. A man who had betrayed her by breaking her confidence and publishing it in his paper. It seems that all journalists were... well, maybe it was better she didn't even think it, but they were.

"Tony, I am so sorry. Has this come from the police? Has there been any more evidence?"

"No, the police haven't contacted me since that day we were there together. I went into work only to be presented with this. I was asked to leave. People shouted at me in the streets and I was chased out of the newsagents on the high street." Tony rested his arms on the table and lay his head on them.

Lola didn't know what to do. She could see that Tyson was on one side of Tony and Sassy on the other. Both of the dogs were leaning against him trying to offer support. However, he didn't seem to even know that they were there.

"Can you help the Tony man?" Tyson asked, his big brown eyes looking so sad.

Lola nodded. She was certainly going to do her best but she suspected that Danny Peterson was involved in this somehow. What could she do, how could she turn back the clock and reclaim Tony's reputation?

Lola thought it was too late. Once this sort of news was out there was nothing anyone could do. Tony's life would never be the same again.

THE RACE IS ON

$\mathcal{L}$ola knew there was a race now, a race to prove Tony was innocent before the rot set in and his life was truly destroyed. Maybe, if she could prove his innocence quickly, then the news would blow over and he would get his job back. People would once again see him as the good man he was.

"Why so sad?" Sassy asked as they walked back along the street.

"Some horrible people have told lies about Tony. Now other people think he is bad and it means he has lost his job."

"Then he can come walking with us more often," Sassy said turning her head and giving a big smile.

"If only it was that easy." Lola felt as if she had let him down. Maybe, if she had found John Smith quicker, then this would never have got quite so out of hand.

"People funny, anyone can smell that Tony is not bad." Sassy was trotting along the path in front of them. To her, the matter was closed. Tony was a good man, she could tell it and she couldn't comprehend how complicated things could get. Once again, Lola envied the little dog.

Lola decided to go back to Tanya's house so she could talk to Wayne. Maybe he could find something out for her. As they passed the church, she saw Father Jackson changing the timing in the noticeboard.

"Good morning, Father," Lola said.

He turned and it was obvious that he was struggling to sleep. However, he put a smile on his face. "Good morning, Lola, and little Sassy, how are you doing?"

"We have just been to see Tony. I feel awful for him, is there anything you can do?"

The priest shook his head. "I wish that there was. I know that Tony didn't do this but he is hiding something. I've felt it for a while and at first, I thought it was a good thing because he often had a smile on his face. Recently, however, I worry about what it could be."

Lola felt the familiar excitement in her gut when she recognized something important. "When did you first notice this?"

"It was not long after he got Tyson. At first, I thought it was the dog making him so happy. He was also so busy and his car was out a few nights. I guess I just thought he was out with the dog but now I'm not so sure."

"Do you have any idea what it could be?" Lola asked.

"No, I know he didn't kill Alexander Petrov, but I get the awful feeling that he's lying about where he was on the night of the murder. What could it mean?"

"I don't know, but do me a favor, do not mention this to anyone if you can help it." Lola wanted to say especially to Daniel Peterson. However, she realized that the priest couldn't hide this fact if he was directly asked.

"Don't worry, I believe in Tony and I will do what I feel is best for him."

Lola continued on her walk and waited until she was around the corner so the father couldn't hear her. "Have you noticed anything different about Tony?" she asked Sassy.

"I think he has a lady friend."

"What makes you think that? Lola asked.

Sassy's eyes were wide and she shook her head in disbelief. "Can't you smell it?"

"Smell?"

"I forget your nose deficient. I could smell her. I should've asked Tyson, he would know."

Lola couldn't remember ever seeing Tony with a girlfriend. Of course, it didn't mean that he didn't have one, or maybe he had recently found one. This fit with his behavior. Tony was a shy man, not the sort to brag about his conquests. But still, if his new lady friend was his alibi, then surely, he would have mentioned her?

Lola was back at Tanya's house. For a moment, she turned and looked out across the countryside. Tanya's house was called Hillview, or 5 The Edge.

From the front of the property, there was a spectacular view out over the Lincolnshire countryside. Lincolnshire was well known as being a flat county. There was little in the way of hills which made it ideal for agriculture.

Spread out before her was a patchwork quilt of farm-land. Green fields of different shades lined by the darker green and brown of the hedgerows and splashed with trees and the occasional blue of a pond.

Lola sighed and turned back to the house, it was pretty as a picture with whitewashed walls and a blue door. A pink rose grew along the front wall draping over the windows. Even though she had only been here several months it felt like home. Was that why she was refusing to use her trust fund to continue the work on her own property?

It was something she needed to look at. Had she become so attached to Tanya and Wayne that she didn't want to move? No, she wouldn't do that. The couple deserved their privacy even though she knew they did not resent her presence. Anyway, this was a question for another day, today she had to see what she could find out about Tony.

When Lola entered the house, Wayne and Tanya were watching an old black and white movie. They looked up and smiled as she came into the room but once more, Lola felt as if she was intruding. She really had to get a grip of herself and decide what to do about her property. She either had to move in as it was and then do the renovations while she was there or come to terms with using her trust fund.

Just for a moment, a picture of her mother's face crossed her mind. It was never her mother smiling, it was always that brokenhearted angry look that haunted her.

"Are you okay?" Tanya asked. "Come on in, sit down and join us with this popcorn."

Lola smiled. Tanya always had a way of making things right. She was almost as good a friend as Sassy.

"I wish I could, unfortunately... well, have you seen the local paper?"

Tanya shook her head. "No, but I can pull it up on my phone if you want."

Before Lola could say any more she was already scrolling across the screen of her phone. The look of shock on her face let Lola know that she found it quickly.

"I can't believe this, Wayne, look at this." Tanya showed him the phone.

Wayne got to his feet, grabbed the phone, and came towards Lola. "How is he?" Wayne asked.

"He's not good, he lost his job, and he's hiding in his house. Apparently, people shouted at him in the street."

Tanya was next to them too, pulling Lola into a hug. "I'm so sorry, I know he's a good man and I know you were trying to help him. What can we do?"

While she was saying all this, Tanya guided them into the kitchen, and before Lola even knew it had happened, they were sitting at the kitchen table and Tanya was making drinks.

"Can you find anything out?" Lola asked Wayne.

Wayne shrugged. "It's not my case..." He must've noticed the way Lola's face fell. "But I can nip into the station for a file I forgot. If no one's around I could possibly look on Daniel's desk."

"I would be really grateful," Lola said. "But don't get into any trouble. The last thing I need to do is get you..." She couldn't finish the sentence for suddenly she was going to say fired.

"Don't worry, I'm a big boy and can look after myself."

Tanya put three coffee cups on the table and sat down with them. Lola felt guilty for asking her boyfriend to put himself in jeopardy for her and for Tony.

"It's okay," Tanya said, obviously seeing the worry on her face. "Wayne wouldn't be the detective he is if he allowed such injustice to go unchallenged."

Lola felt tears prickle at the back of her eyes. Sassy leaned against her leg and sent loving thoughts into her mind. "It's all right, I just want to say thank you, thank you so much for being such good friends."

"Let's just hope I can find something," Wayne said.

Lola felt such a sense of dread. She was sure that Danny Boy Peterson had informed the press, knowing that once Tony was guilty in the eyes of the people that his life would never be the same again.

THE WAITING GAME

*A*s soon as Wayne had left for the station, Lola felt guilty. Tanya worked really hard and sometimes even had to work weekends. She managed a large art gallery in Lincoln and Wayne was a police detective. It was very rare that the two of them got a weekend off together and here was Lola, disturbing that precious time and putting Wayne's job in danger.

"Stop it!" Tanya said.

"Hmm?" Lola replied pretending that she didn't understand.

"Don't even," Tanya said. "It's written all over your face, you're feeling guilty for disturbing mine and Wayne's weekend but don't. You know what sort of person he is, that I am. Do you think either of us could sit idly by while Tony's life was being destroyed?"

"I guess not. I just wish I could've done something myself earlier. After all, Uri Petrov did give me a list of suspects, and I have hardly even looked into them."

"Well, maybe we could do some research now?"

Lola wondered about that. She had in fact, already looked them up on the Internet. There wasn't much that she could find out about them. She had been going to speak to Tilly, not that she expected even Tilly would know about Russian gangsters in the city. It was just that once Tony was set free, other cases took over and she kind of forgot.

Sassy was leaning against her leg offering support. Lola reached down and scratched behind her ears. "I'm not stressed, just a little anxious."

"I here, if you need me," Sassy said.

Lola bent over and kissed her between her ears. Sassy reached up and licked Lola's cheek.

"Can I be a princess now?" Sassy asked and then sat down wiggling her little butt and grinning up at Lola.

"Okay," Lola said and stood up and crossed the room. In a little basket on the counter by the door was a plastic sparkling dog tiara. Lola felt her cheeks heating as she knew that Tanya must think she was crazy. With all that was going on, here she was fitting her Frenchie with her dog tiara before letting her out into the garden.

Sassy was sitting waiting but finding it incredibly hard to keep still. The tiara had been bought a short while ago after next door's cat called herself Princess Portia Ebony Blaze and said that dogs were stupid. Sassy had taken it upon herself to prove to Portia that she was every bit as regal as the cat was.

Portia wasn't impressed and had taken to hiding from Sassy so as not to acknowledge what Sassy called her Princessness.

Lola fitted the tiara with some trouble as the little Frenchie wouldn't keep still. Once it was on, she opened the door. Sassy ran out into the back garden searching high and low for the errant black cat.

"You and that dog are something special," Tanya said.

"It cheers me up!" Lola shrugged before grabbing her laptop. She quickly gave Tanya the rundown of what she had found out about the suspects that Alexander

Petrov's brother had given her. "I guess I didn't forget them altogether because I managed to rule two of them out," Lola said as she opened her laptop.

Quickly, she scrolled to the documents and opened the one she was looking for. "Yeah, here we go. Maxine and Ivan Popov were out of the country at the time of Alexander's death. They are rival drug dealers and so they would've had a beef with him. I know it's possible that they had someone else kill him but I don't think so. They have a factory unit with lots of heavy machinery and a cutter that could be the murder weapon, but I don't see any reason for them to come after Alexander. He was small fry as far as they are concerned and with his father…"

"I knew you wouldn't have just forgotten this," Tanya said. "Now, why don't you think they were involved?"

"Well, looking into this, Alexander was small fry as far as they were concerned and I believe his father's reputation would've put them off." *Of course, if they knew that his father was dying maybe they decided to make a statement*, Lola thought.

"What were you thinking, just then? Tanya asked.

Lola explained about Borya Petrov's cancer and how she was sure that he was dying.

"That might change a lot of things," Tanya said.

"I know, it certainly does change things." Lola wondered if it gave her another suspect. She had an idea, one she would follow up on later.

"And the other suspects?"

Lola shook her head. "My sources, and I don't have that many, couldn't tell me much about the other two. One is a man named Pavel. My sources have heard of him, they don't know his last name and they don't know how to find him. They are afraid of him and they don't want to go looking. The other is a man named Asseney Lebedev. He used to work for Borya but the two fell out. I haven't managed to find out why and I haven't managed to find anything that points at him having anything to do with this. I guess I could ask Borya if he could be involved." Lola didn't want to do that.

"Why don't you?" Tanya asked.

"Because if I do, I might put a target on his back."

Lola's phone rang and it was Wayne. "Hey, did you find anything?"

"Did I ever!" Wayne said. "It's bedlam here. I don't think they know I've seen them but you have to get to Tony. Danny has had another tipoff, he has officers getting ready and a search warrant in hand. He is going to search the shed of the churchyard and he believes that both Tony and Father Jackson were involved in the murder."

Lola couldn't believe her ears. What could they be looking for? It didn't matter, something told her that she had to get to that shed before the police did, but if they were already on the way could she make it?

"Thanks, Wayne, I have to go."

"Good luck," he said.

TROUBLE IS COMING

"*I* have to go," Lola said.

"I understand. I pray that this will turn out the way it should," Tanya said.

Lola was already up and running to the door. She called Sassy. Sometimes the little Frenchie would play a bit of a game. She didn't always like to be caught and she would run away and force Lola to chase her. However, she must've understood the urgency in Lola's voice as she came racing up the garden as quick as she could and leaped into Lola's waiting arms.

Lola kissed her, quickly pulled off the tiara, and grabbed her keys as she was walking to the door, she fitted the

Frenchie's harness. Soon they were both strapped into the car and on their way to Tony's.

As they passed the church, Lola slammed on the brakes and pulled the Land Rover Discovery into the curb. She could see Tony and Father Jackson picking dead branches up off the graves. Tyson was lying under a tree and looked to be asleep.

The trees often shed branches and bits of sticks and Tony kept the churchyard tidy by moving them out of the way. It looked like the father was either helping him or talking to him while he worked.

Lola ran over to them trying to decide what she should say.

"Lola, is there a problem?" Father Jackson asked, his eyebrows raised at the speed she was coming.

Lola took a breath. "I've been reliably informed that the police are on their way to search the toolshed in your churchyard. I don't know what they're looking for, but I'm worried."

"Hey, when did you get here?" Tyson's voice was clear in Lola's head.

"I really don't understand," Father Jackson said. "The shed's full of old tools and a lot of junk that really needs clearing out. We must get around to that one day."

"We in hurry, trouble coming," Sassy said to Tyson.

Sometimes it could be hard for Lola to concentrate when she was listening to several different conversations and the last thing she needed at the moment was to be confused. "Maybe we should go and see if there's anything to find?"

"I hate trouble," Tyson said. "Tony man worried, I hate him to be worried. He too good to be worried."

"I assure you there isn't," Tony said. "However, the thought of the police causing any more trouble, and causing trouble for you, Father, I just can't bear it. Perhaps I should just go?"

"I chase trouble and bite it." Sassy snapped her teeth and jumped at nothing.

"Well, at least show me the shed first," Lola said.

"Oh, I couldn't do that." Tyson bowed his head and his tail dropped between his legs. "I'd get into trouble, I hate it when the stick comes out."

"There won't be any stick," Lola said to Tyson and then realized that Tony and Father Jackson were staring at her.

"To throw," Lola said and shrugged her shoulders, she had to learn to shut out the dogs when she was around people.

"I should go," Tony said again.

"No, you're not going anywhere. You are innocent, I know it. But, yes, yes, that's a really good idea, let's look at the shed." Father Jackson turned and led the way and both Lola, Tony, and the two dogs followed.

For once the dogs were being quite subdued rather than racing around as they would normally be. Lola understood that they were concerned too and that they would do anything to help Tony. Maybe she could use a nose at some point, she just couldn't understand how, at least not at the moment.

Lola was listening for the sound of sirens, but so far she had heard none. Every fiber of her being wanted to rush. She wanted time to search the shed to see what the police might be looking for.

What would you do if you find evidence that he's guilty? No, she pushed that thought aside, but why else would she need to look in the shed? Lola trusted her gut, and it told her that Tony was innocent. It also told her that Daniel Peterson wouldn't care. If he could find anything to tie Tony to the Russian then he would.

"Has Alexander ever been in the shed?" Lola asked, suddenly wondering if that was where this tied in.

"Not that I'm aware of," Father Jackson said and Tony was shaking his head.

"No, I've never seen him in the shed," Tony said. "He used to do his dealing along the back wall there where the trees are." He pointed across the churchyard to where a footpath ran along one side. "We were always chasing him off. The man had no respect, dealing drugs in a churchyard."

Father Jackson chuckled. "Now, now, Tony, he was just outside of the churchyard. However, it did make me very angry. I consider all of this village to be my people, even those who don't visit the church."

They had arrived at the shed and Tony opened the door. Lola noticed it wasn't locked, however, there was a lock and a clasp on the outside and she could see that there was a padlock on the floor.

"Who has keys to the padlock?" she asked.

"That would be me and Father Jackson," Tony said. "I don't think there's anyone else is there?"

"No, I don't think so. However, those keys are very old. The lock was fitted before I arrived in the parish and that was many, many years ago. I also don't really hide them, they are often just inside the church."

Lola stepped through the door and into the brick-built shed. It was about 15' x 15' and had an earth floor. It looked rather ramshackle and old, with only the middle looking organized where there was a mower, a hedge trimmer, and various other gardening tools. Along one side were stacks and stacks of chairs, some of them looked as if they were usable and others looked as if they hadn't been touched in years. There were two or three big garden umbrellas. What looked like an old swing leaned against the sidewall and a hammock that looked as if the string part had rotted away.

"Micey!" Sassy said coming into the little shed, sniffing along the floor. Her head was down, her tail raised high, and wagging constantly she searched the ground where the mice had been.

"You don't have any poison down, do you? I think Sassy had sniffed out a mouse." Lola asked quickly. The last thing she needed was for Sassy to find some poison and eat it before she had a chance to stop her.

"No, don't worry," Tony said. "I don't like to poison them."

There were boxes piled everywhere, some closed, some open with magazines, books, and clothes piling out of them. Along the back wall of the shed, it was hard to discern what was stored there. They looked like home-made banners and pieces of wood with writing on and all sorts of painted bits and pieces many of which looked like they hadn't been moved in years. Lola's heart sank. She wasn't going to find whatever the police were looking for; it would take her forever.

At least they hadn't arrived yet, or so she thought, she hadn't heard the sound of sirens or cars pulling up.

Her heart nearly jumped into her throat.

"What's going on here?" Daniel Peterson asked.

How had he crept up on them and what was she going to say to explain why she was here?

THE RAID

S assy barked at Peterson and he stepped back raising his hands and lifting his foot as if to kick her. Lola stepped in between her and him and scooped Sassy up into her arms.

"Get in here and arrest these people," Peterson said.

PC Jenkins had just walked into the shed and was shaking his head. "What for?"

"They were tampering with evidence, obviously trying to destroy evidence." Daniel had his hands on his hips and was glaring at the young PC as if he was dense.

Lola chuckled and saw the flash of annoyance cross Peterson's face. She wasn't backing down. "What on earth are you talking about?" she asked, knowing that the best course of action was to pretend that she had just been there to see Tony.

"We have a search warrant to search the shed and here you are trying to destroy evidence," Peterson said.

"Well, I believe you will find that Tony and Father Jackson were working in the churchyard and I was just taking little Sassy for a walk." Lola held Sassy out a little from her to make sure they saw her.

Sassy growled and nipped at Peterson. The man flinched and stepped back.

"I saw these two, and like most people would do, I stopped to say hello." Lola hoped that they hadn't noticed her Discovery parked outside the church. If she was walking the dog, surely she would walk from the house?

"That's a likely story, you will have all been colluding in the shed we're about to search. No doubt hoping to destroy evidence."

"What evidence?" Lola glanced at the disordered mess and chuckled.

Peterson glared at PC Jenkins once more. "If you won't arrest them at least take them outside."

Lola held up her hand. "May I see the search warrant?"

The scowl that crossed Peterson's face did not improve his looks, but he reached into his pocket and pulled out a folded piece of paper. He took the time to smirk before he handed it to her.

Lola put Sassy down and opened the paper. It gave him the right to search the shed and to seize anything pertinent that he found there. It did not give him the right to go into the church.

"What is it?" Father Jackson asked.

Lola noticed that Tyson was cowering in the corner, that Sassy was sitting in front of him, protecting him from the shouting as much as she could. "It looks in order. Tony, Father Jackson, we should wait outside. Sassy, Tyson, come on."

They all went outside and sat on one of the benches as ½ dozen police officers all in white forensic overalls entered the shed. It was a horrible thing to see and made you feel as if something awful was going to happen.

Lola had been surprised at how geared up the team was. Peterson was pushing this to the limit but who could have told him there was something in the shed? And what could they be looking for?

"I don't want to lose Tony man," Tyson said and Lola could see that Sassy was trying to comfort him. How could she help without making herself sound crazy?

"I really hate how this is scaring Tyson," Tony said. "I wonder if we should ask Alice to come and take him again?"

"I think that's a really good idea. Why don't I go and meet her down by the street?" Lola said.

"I don't think the officers will want you walking off," Father Jackson said.

"I'm sure they won't mind if I don't go far; after all, it's not me that they're looking at." Lola shook her head and wished she hadn't said that, however, she wanted a few moments alone with Tyson.

"She's right," Tony said. "Thank you so much."

Lola asked the officer if he minded if she arranged for the dog to be taken. He said that was fine as long as she stayed in his line of sight. Lola quickly rang Alice and asked her to come down and meet her and then she put Tyson on a lead and left Sassy with Tony and walked down to the street.

"I'm really worried about Tony man," Tyson said. "If I'd been braver, maybe I could save him. Maybe I don't deserve someone like Tony man."

Lola knelt down and stroked the big dog's soft head. He had such large expressive brown eyes and she looked into them deeply wanting him to understand how much she cared for him. "You listen to me. Tony is very lucky to have a dog as wonderful as you and I am going to make sure that I do everything I can to keep him safe. You are very brave. You were brave to stay there when you were afraid but promise me you will never jump up or bite that horrible man."

"Not even to save Tony man?"

"No, because it would hurt Tony really badly if you were taken from him and if you did that you would be. Alice is going to look after you for a while. I don't know how long for but don't worry, Tony is going to be all right."

Tyson leaned against her and Lola put her arms around him and pulled him in close. He had the softest silkiest coat she had ever felt. "Don't worry, Alice will look after you."

"I like Alice too, I like you too. I never knew life could be this good."

Once Alice had collected Tyson, Lola wandered back and sat on the bench once more. The police were busy taking photos and then taking things out of the shed. They had created quite a large pile.

"Well, it looks like we're going to get the shed sorted for us," Father Jackson chuckled. "Once they're gone, I'm only putting half of this stuff back."

"If you ever need any help, I'm free some weekends," PC Jenkins said.

"Thank you very much, son," Father Jackson said. "Any offers of help are always appreciated."

They sat and watched as more and more stuff was removed from the shed. The chairs were all piled up as well as the umbrellas and the hammock. All the tools were put in a different pile and the boxes and boxes of what looked like old toys and clothes. Now they seemed to be moving the bits of painted board.

"What are they for?" Lola asked.

"They haven't been used in years," Father Jackson said. "The children used to put on plays and they were part of the sets. Now I wish I had been able to donate them or get rid of them. If all this rubbish is cleared out there will be so much room in that shed."

"Maybe I should be accused of a crime more often?" Tony said and chuckled. "This is so ridiculous, but like you say, at least we're getting some work done."

They were all chuckling now for it did seem ridiculous. The dust and cobwebs on some of the items they were bringing out made it quite obvious that they hadn't been moved in months if not years. Lola was starting to relax and she could see and hear that Peterson was getting more and more stressed.

He had been shouting at the officers to take care, to move this, to do that. The officers themselves were looking pretty fed up. The only one who seemed happy was Sassy, who was sitting on Tony's knee getting cuddles. That was something she could cope with all day.

Lola was starting to get bored and she could really do with a drink. "PC Jenkins, do you mind if we make some drinks?"

"That is a fabulous idea," Father Jackson said, "I can go make them, and if you want one, Jenkins, I don't mind."

Jenkins looked at the shed and the people going in and out and cataloging all the equipment. "I can't see a problem and I could kill a coffee."

Just as Father Jackson got up, there was a shout of excitement from Daniel Peterson.

"We have him!"

SECRET ROOM

*D*etective Daniel Peterson came out of the shed with a look of glee on his face. He was already pulling out his handcuffs as he approached them.

"What is going on?" Lola asked.

Peterson pushed past her and pulled Tony to his feet causing Sassy to have to jump to the ground. As she landed she spun around and grabbed onto his trousers shaking them for all she was worth and growling her displeasure.

"Sassy, no," Lola said and tried to pick the little Frenchie up.

Peterson was hopping on one leg and trying to both kick out at Sassy and avoid her at the same time. If it hadn't been so serious it would've been quite hilarious. Lola managed to grab hold of the errant Frenchie and picked her up. Sassy was still growling and tried to leap from her arms.

"You're not helping," Lola whispered into her ear.

"Don't like him," Sassy said. And then growled before letting out a high-pitched screech that had Daniel hopping backward.

"Control that dog or I'll have it taken away under the Dangerous Dogs Act," Daniel said.

"You scared her," Lola said.

"He did not!" Sassy said and growled once more.

Peterson could see that Sassy was now contained and so he turned his attention back to Tony. "I knew you had done it, I just didn't know how sick you were. Tony Munch, I am arresting you for the murder of Alexander Petrov. Turn around." Peterson slapped handcuffs on Tony and dragged him away toward the car while reading him his rights.

"What is going on?" Father Peterson asked of one of the PCs.

"I'm sorry, Father, it looks like Mr. Munch had a... well, a shrine, or a room dedicated to the destruction of Alexander Petrov. There were pictures of him and all sorts. It's very damning."

"Hey, you," Peterson shouted as he came back to them. "You don't tell people what we found; this is a crime scene." Peterson was shaking his head and grabbing the PC's arm, turning him around and pushing him back into the shed. "You two had better go; don't let me catch you sniffing around here again."

Father Jackson raised his eyebrows and cleared his throat. Peterson paused and had the decency to look a little bit abashed.

"This is my churchyard, Detective, and you will treat it with respect."

The father turned and walked away and Lola followed him. "Did you know anything about that room?" Lola asked when they were out of range.

"I knew it was there, but it hasn't been used in years. I also do not believe that Tony did whatever they say he did. Most of the time when he is here at the church I'm here with him and he wouldn't have time to clear out all that rubbish and get in that room. However, we both did think that the other one had done some sorting in the shed a couple of weeks ago. In fact, it was about a week before Alexander's body was found. I do not know what is going on but I know a good man when I see one. What are we going to do?"

"Can you remember anything specific about that time?" Lola asked.

Father Jackson looked away into the distance and then shook his head. "Not really... oh, wait a moment. It was shortly after that when Tony noticed his book was missing. I'm sure it must be a coincidence. This is just all so worrying... and all I can think to do is pray on the matter."

"I will talk to Patricia Darnell again, she is a good solicitor she will be able to tell us what to do. However, if Tony is hiding something we need to know what it is."

Father Jackson agreed and then said his goodbyes. Lola noticed that he looked very tired as he walked away. The stress he was feeling must've been awful. Not as bad as what Tony must be feeling, though. How could she prove he was innocent?

* * *

Lola walked back to her car and fastened Sassy to the seat. What could she do? Leaning back she closed her eyes to think. She had to have missed something. There had to be a clue... and yet, she couldn't seem to find it.

Sassy pawed her arm. Lola opened her eyes and looked at the little Frenchie. There was obvious worry on her little wrinkled face. "Where they take Tony?" Sassy asked.

"To the police station."

"Is that like the pound?"

"Yes, I suppose it is a little. Don't worry, we'll get him out."

Sassy sent a feeling of warmth and love into Lola's mind. The little dog trusted her and believed she could do this. She was not going to let her down. Pulling out her phone she dialed Patricia Darnell's number. It went straight to voicemail. "You have reached Patricia Darnell. I'm currently in court. Leave me a message and I will get back to you as soon as I can."

Lola left a quick message explaining what had happened. On the last visit to the station, Patricia had told Danny Boy that Lola was her assistant. It meant she would have the right to speak to Tony and so she decided to go straight to the station. He would have been booked in by now and she could talk to him before his temper got out of control and he said something he shouldn't.

What could she do? Though she knew she had to do something she felt that this had got out of hand. Tony was arrested, she had no leads and she had no idea how to find any. Things were looking bad and even though she believed in the justice system, she knew that sometimes good people were found guilty. Sometimes, the innocent went to jail.

THE EVIDENCE

*L*ola waited in the corridor of the police station. She knew that Daniel Peterson was deliberately keeping her waiting but there was nothing she could do about it. She had sent a text to Wayne and he said he would see her as soon as he could. Lola doubted he could do anything to help, but his support would be something.

"This place boring," Sassy said.

"Why don't you go to sleep?" The little Frenchie was curled up on Lola's lap and had been watching people come and go. At first, she had been intrigued with the different smells of the different people but as time went by and nothing more happened all she wanted to do was sleep.

"Okay." With that, Sassy tucked her nose beneath her rear paws and was almost instantly snoring.

Lola envied the little dog. It seemed that she could sleep anywhere at the drop of a hat, whereas, sleep was something that Lola still struggled with. Often, she would toss and turn at night knowing that when she slipped into sleep her memories would wake her. Since she had Sassy, she rarely woke up screaming. The little dog could tell when her dreams were getting bad and would either send loving thoughts or if that didn't work, she would wake Lola.

It hadn't stopped the dreams, but it had reduced them by a big percentage. It was also much nicer to not wake up screaming. That tended to scare everyone in the house, and Lola hated having to explain it, or having to cope with the looks of sympathy. The past was best left in the past.

Lola had been offered counseling when she came back from Afghanistan. At the time, she didn't think she needed it but when she looked back she wondered if that had been her real motivation for turning it down. Part of her believed that she deserved these nightmares. That it was her punishment for leaving her parents and never patching up the argument that broke their hearts, Or, that it was her punishment for surviving when many of her team didn't.

"You here," Sassy said in Lola's mind.

It always amazed Lola that the little dog could sense the dark thoughts whenever they clouded Lola's mind, even while she slept. It didn't matter what Sassy was doing, if Lola needed her she was there. "Yes, I'm here." Lola pulled her mind away from the past, from the bad place as Sassy called it.

Daniel Peterson walked down the corridor, well actually, he sauntered. His head was high and he made sure not to make eye contact with Lola as he passed. It was obvious posturing and if the situation had not been so serious Lola would have chuckled. However, she had the feeling that he was up to something and that whatever it was it would not be good

Intuition had kept her alive more than once. Her breath caught in her throat and she felt her heart kick up a beat or two. What was happening now?

On her lap, Sassy was now awake. She sat up and leaned against her. Lola put her arms around the little dog and held her close just as the door opened in the corridor.

Peterson was back, and this time Father Jackson was with him. Though he was trying to look brave, he looked confused and possibly a little annoyed.

"Father Jackson, are you all right?" Lola asked.

"Yes, yes, I'm just here to answer a few questions."

"Would you like me to be with you?"

A look of relief came over the father's face and he nodded. "Yes, that would be most helpful."

The look that crossed Daniel's face was not relief and for a moment, she thought he was going to deny her request. Instead, he shrugged his shoulders and indicated down the corridor.

Putting Sassy down, Lola followed them, checking her phone quickly to see if Patricia had answered. There was nothing; should she try and get another solicitor? The problem was she knew no one, and all she had to do was make sure that Tony said nothing until Patricia arrived.

Daniel took them into an interview room. Lola and Father Jackson took the seats on one side. Daniel dragged out the chair causing it to scrape across the room. This seemed to be one of his main tactics. Lola hated to admit it, but it had an effect. The scraping sound set your nerves on edge and the detective knew that if you were on edge you were more likely to make a mistake.

Often, people gave things away by talking and wanting to fill the silence. All she had to do was get Father Jackson to say very little or nothing and the same with Tony until Patricia could arrive.

Peterson sat down. "Tell me about the secret room."

Father Jackson's eyes opened wide and his mouth fell open.

"I think we should maybe wait until Patricia Darnell gets here," Lola said.

"Well, if you have something to hide then I guess you'd better." Danny Boy chuckled a little and crossed his arms over the folder on the desk.

Sassy growled and barked, pulling Peterson's attention to her. Lola was pleased that he still looked nervous.

"Control that dog," he shrieked in a most unmanly fashion.

"She senses stress, it is her job. Take your time, Father, and do not worry."

Father Jackson took a breath and looked much calmer. "We have nothing to hide," he said shaking his head to emphasize the point. "That is not a secret room, it is just a room that hasn't been opened in a lot of years."

"Really!" Daniel removed his arms from the folder and opened it slowly. Without looking at either of them he pulled out a photo and then slammed it down hard on the table. "Then what is this?"

Lola felt her stomach turn. This was bad, this was damning. She could see from the look in Father Jackson's eyes that he believed it too. Surely, Tony could not have done this?

A WALL OF DOUBT

*L*ola stared at the photo. It was a picture of one wall in the hidden room, of that she was sure. On the wall were various photos of Alexander Petrov. They looked like surveillance photos. As if someone had been stalking him for some time. There were some of him at the back of the churchyard dealing drugs. There were some of him in town. Some during the day, some at night. One showed him with a fashion model, not his fiancée.

Had Tony really taken these? It made no sense. Or did it? If he really did hate the Russian, if he really hated what the man was doing, had he been documenting it? If he had, then surely he was doing it to take to the police.

Daniel chuckled and was sorting through the photos in the folder. They were all face down so they couldn't see them but they had numbers on the back. He found the one he wanted, pulled it out of the folder, and with a flourish slammed it down on the table next to the previous one.

Lola fought hard to stop her nerves from kicking in and the bang did not make her jump. Externally at least. Sassy was leaning against her leg offering as much support as she could. Father Jackson, on the other hand, did jump and he also let out a little gasp.

These new photos showed more pictures of Alexander Petrov. Only on these, he was splashed with red. Someone had carved out his eyes on one photo. On another, there was an ax pasted onto the picture. The way it was placed it looked like it was chopping off his leg and red marker was scrawled all over the photos.

"So, do you still think Mr. Munch is innocent?"

"Of course, I do," Father Jackson said without hesitation. "I do not know what to say or who put these there but I do know that it wasn't Tony."

Lola was pleased that the father hadn't hesitated in denying this. He believed in Tony and he stood by him.

These were rare qualities in the modern world and they gave her hope. However, the evidence was damning and she for once was speechless.

"Well, Miss Ramsey, don't you have anything to say for yourself?" Danny asked.

Her mind was whirling trying to think.

"Was there any sniffy of Tony in that room?" Sassy asked.

That was a good point, this was all circumstantial. "You have the photos," Lola said. "What evidence do you have that they were placed there by Tony?"

"We have enough." Danny said but she could see that the question had annoyed him. It was a start, now all she had to do was find out what this meant.

"Unless you are holding us, we would like to go now. When Patricia gets here we would like to see everything you have and then we would like to speak to Tony. Until then, Tony will not be answering any questions."

"We'll see about that, if he wants to talk he can talk. And you know what Tony's temper is like!" Daniel said.

"In that case, I would like to see Tony now," Lola said.

Daniel spread out a few more photos on the table and then picked them all up. "That can be arranged. Would you like to see him too, Father Jackson?"

"Yes, that would be nice."

"Then wait here, I will bring him to you. My own theory, if you want to hear it, is that you are in on this with him, Father Jackson. We have a lot of evidence from that shed, including your mobiles. Don't you worry, I will be watching you too."

With that, Daniel walked out of the room.

"What does he mean?" Father Jackson asked. "My mobile is in my pocket. How did this happen?"

Lola didn't know what to say. All she could do was try to firefight until Patricia got here. She just hoped it wouldn't be too long.

Tony was shown into the interview room. The poor man looked terrible. There was a paleness to his skin and his eyes were sunken. His trousers were hanging a little loose as his belt had been removed and his trainers flopped about on his feet as his laces had also been taken.

Lola knew that this was standard procedure, but she also knew that it was a way off both protecting the suspect and dehumanizing them. Poor Tony must feel awful.

Sassy ran straight over to him tugging the lead out of Lola's hands. Tony scooped her up into his arms and hugged her close. "How is Tyson doing?"

"Don't worry, he's with Alice and she's looking after him well," Lola said.

"Father Jackson, you have to go and don't come back. I swear I did not do this but tell the police that you knew nothing. The last thing I want to do is bring you or the church into disrepute."

"There, there, Tony. What sort of Christian would I be if I did that? We are going to beat this. I promise!"

"Have they questioned you?" Lola asked.

"Yes, but I told them I wouldn't speak until Patricia was with me. I don't mind speaking with you here either," he said smiling at Lola.

"Thank you, but I think it's best we wait until Patricia gets here."

"They showed me some pictures. I didn't take them and I don't know how they got there." Tony turned his eyes to Father Jackson. "You think that is when we thought the shed had been tided?"

"I do, but I don't know how we can use this."

"Tony, when you were asked for an alibi, we both thought you were hiding something. If you were, right now we need to know what it was," Lola said.

Tony looked a little abashed. Color flooded his cheeks and he ducked his head to hide it.

"Come on now, son, if this is something embarrassing it doesn't matter. You need to tell us where you were," Father Jackson said.

"What if I was committing a sin?" Tony asked.

THE SINNER

*L*ola drew in a breath. Was he about to confess?

"Tony, good man," Lola heard in her mind. Sassy was staring straight at her as if she was insisting that she was believed.

Lola nodded. It didn't matter, whatever this confession was they had to know. If Tony really was guilty then they had to know that too. However, she really hoped he wasn't.

"There are sins and there are sins," Father Jackson said. "I know you, Tony, and you can tell me the truth. I promise I will not think the worst of you."

Tony looked from Lola to Father Jackson and then down at the table. It was as if he was trying to decide what to say, or how to say it. Then he looked up and the words just blurted out of him. "I was at the Avenue hotel, with Maureen Cooper." His hands flew to his face, as if in an attempt to stop the words but it was too late.

Lola let out a breath of relief, but she could see Father Jackson's brow was furrowed and his mouth hung open slightly. Why was he concerned?

"Were you meeting Mrs. Cooper for a private liaison?" Father Jackson asked.

Ah, that was what Tony was ashamed of, he had been with a married woman. Lola was surprised, Tony was so meek and nice she couldn't imagine this of him but it could have been much worse.

Tony blushed so red that his ears appeared to glow and he lowered his head, nodding. "I'm sorry, Father, but I like her a lot and her husband is so cold and distant."

"Will Mrs. Cooper provide you with an alibi?" Father Jackson asked.

"I haven't asked her, I haven't seen her since this all got so silly." Tony was still blushing and seemed unable to meet their eyes.

Lola was excited. This was how they could get Tony out of this mess. "This is good, I appreciate that she may be a married woman, and I appreciate that it is a sin, but these things happen and as she can exonerate you, then we have to tell Detective Peterson... now," Lola said.

"I think we need to think about this," Father Jackson said. "If it can be done discreetly then I agree we should tell him. However, I do not think that Daniel Peterson would be discrete and with the elections coming up there is a lot that could be lost here."

Lola was confused. "Elections? Who is Mrs. Cooper?"

"She's the wife of counselor Stephen Cooper. A man who is a good friend of mine, I may say," Father Jackson said.

"I'm sorry, Father, Stephen treats her so badly and we have talked about her separation. Maureen just wanted to wait until after the election. Though she no longer loves her husband and feels he no longer loves her, she still cares for him and she loves what he stands for. She does not want to see his reputation damaged. That is why I haven't said anything and that is why we would rather not say anything until after the election." Tony shrugged, his cheeks were no longer glowing but he did still look a little embarrassed.

"Do you have any idea who could have killed Alexander?" Lola asked.

Both men shook their heads.

"Well, we can hold Mrs. Cooper in the background for now. We need to look at who would benefit from Alexander's death. We know that Daniel Peterson is going to say that both of you would do so." Lola looked from Tony to Father Jackson. "He threatened the lifestyle of the village and the things you cared for by dealing to the locals. By putting the children of the village in danger. We have to look at who else could have gained from his death."

"His father was a hard man," Father Jackson said. "Perhaps Alexander let him down or did something that he didn't like."

"Perhaps you are right," Lola said but she didn't think so. Borya's grief had been too sharp. "Maybe I should go and talk to him again. I just didn't want him to know that Tony was a suspect."

"Why not?" Tony asked.

Lola wished she had not said that. The last thing Tony needed was to know that not only was he a suspect in a murder, but he might have a target on his back. That if the Russian thought he got away with murder, then he might decide to take justice into his own hands.

Tony's mouth fell open and he raised his hands as he realized just that point. "No, no, this can't be happening. There is no way I'm telling anyone about Maureen. Not if there's a possibility that I could put her in danger. Lola, you have to help me. I didn't do this, I promise I didn't do this."

"I believe you," Lola said. "Patricia is in court at the moment, but she has to be out soon. All I can say to you, Tony, is do not say anything until she is with you. When she does come tell her exactly what you told us. You have to trust her."

"I can't, I won't put Maureen at risk.

"I know Borya Petrov, I promise you you will not." Lola knew that she had to go see the Russian again. That if she explained to him then Tony would be fine. Maybe she could get a handle on who had done this.

"Tony, do not lose your temper. Peterson may say things to make you. Think of Tyson and say nothing for him... no matter what."

Tony nodded.

* * *

As Lola was leaving she turned back and looked at Tony. "Remember, don't say anything until Patricia is here. Don't let them make you talk, don't lose your temper."

"I won't, I promise," Tony said.

"Remember the breathing exercises we practiced," Father Jackson added.

Tony nodded. "I've got it... and thank you, thank you both."

The corridor seemed so empty and desolate as they walked along it. The grey and white walls were practical and easy to care for. In places, there were scuffs and dents to attest to the violence these walls had seen. Lola hated the thought of Tony being taken back to a cell. Was he alone? How would he cope for the night?

Her phone rang, jangling her nerves and she almost jumped out of her skin.

"Just phoney," Sassy said.

Lola pulled it out of her pocket. "Lola Ramsey, Private Investigator, how may I help you?"

"It's Patricia Darnell, I just left the court and I'm on my way to the station. I shall be there shortly.

Lola explained that they were just leaving and that they could meet her.

"Meet me at Betty's around 11 am tomorrow, I need to go through the evidence and see what they have on him."

"Will you be able to get him out tonight?" Lola asked. "I have some savings if he needs bail." A vision of her parents' graves flooded her mind and she had to bite back tears.

"Don't worry about that. I won't know until I've seen the evidence and if they wish to charge him. As for bail, police bail is free, he is just required to return to the custody suite when requested."

"That sounds so civilized, custody suite!"

"It's not the Ritz, believe me, but he should be safe."

Lola breathed a sigh of relief, hoping this was the news they needed. Would Patricia be able to get the charges dropped? Somehow, Lola doubted she would. Peterson was a wily fox and the evidence was damming.

GOOSE CHASE

"*D*o you need to go?" Lola asked Sassy.

Father Jackson chuckled. "I wouldn't mind a walk myself, and there's a park not far from here."

"Would be nice," Sassy said.

"Lead the way."

The father turned left and set off down the street. "It is just a few minutes and it's such a nice day. I'm sure the stretch will do us good."

Lola followed him and let Sassy run to the length of her lead. "Tony is very lucky to have you."

"No, not really. He has done so much to help me over the years. He gives generously of his time and without him, the churchyard would be a much poorer place."

"Even so, most people would not put themselves out for another in the way you have."

The father nodded. "You are right, and it is a sad reflection on the modern world. Too often people are judged guilty without a trial. I do worry about a world where justice is played out in the press and not in the courtroom."

Lola had to agree. They walked into the reasonably quiet park and Lola found that Sassy was pulling. Scanning the trees and the path she could not see a squirrel but then the little Frenchie made it to a patch of grass and squatted down to do a wee.

"Ohhh, that is good," Sassy said. "I guess I was getting desperate."

Lola chuckled.

"It looks like she did need to go," Father Jackson said. "You have a very special relationship with that dog. I have seen how tuned into your feelings she is, and how she helps you. She's very clever."

"I am very lucky to have her. I was wondering, would you mind if we went to see Borya Petrov?"

"Is that wise?"

"He helped me before, he desperately wants to find out who killed his son and I feel that he may have resources inside the police. I want to steer him away from Tony and I want to see if he has any other ideas. You can stay outside if you want to."

"I am a man of God, I am happy to accompany you."

Lola, Father Jackson, and Sassy were soon walking into the office of Borya Petrov.

"Miss Ramsey, it is good to see you again, and Father Jackson," Borya said. "Can I offer you some refreshments?"

"Thank you, we won't be staying long, I do not wish to impose too much. I wanted to let you know where I've got to on the case." Lola sat in the chair that Borya indicated. It was off to one side of his office where there was a small seating area with a sofa and three chairs around a glass coffee table. Borya sat opposite them on the sofa and his seat would allow him to look out over the city and enjoy the view.

"I have heard they have a suspect, a good one," Borya said with tension to his voice and Lola noticed a tightness to his jaw.

Lola felt Father Jackson tense beside her and she reached out to touch his arm. "That is correct, but this is a Daniel Peterson suspect, I can assure you he is innocent. He has a cast-iron alibi; however, he did not wish to let Detective Peterson in on it at this time. Peterson, in my opinion, is being led down the garden path to easy town. I believe that the killer left evidence to try to frame the suspect. So I'm here to ask you a few questions if you will let me?"

Lola could see that Borya was clenching his fists and his jaw was tight. He seemed to have aged since she saw him last and despite the makeup, his face was definitely showing a touch of yellow.

"Go ahead."

Lola took in a deep breath. She knew that she was playing with fire, but Sassy left her side and went over to Borya. Once again he picked her up and cuddled her close. It seemed that the Frenchie magic was working even on the tough old Russian.

"Do you have cancer?" Lola asked. *Way to go, ask him gently!*

For a moment, Borya looked annoyed and then his face crumpled and he gave her a slight smile. "Perhaps your little dog knows for she offers me comfort. Yes, I have cancer of the liver. It has spread and I do not have long to live. I would like to see my son's killer punished before I die."

"I am sorry to hear this," Lola said. "Let's make sure that we punish the right person."

Borya nodded. "What can I do to help?"

"I believe that the killer must've known your son very well. They had been following him for some time and had taken many, many photos. I was given a list of people that your son thought could be involved. Would you take a look at it and see what you think?"

"Of course."

Lola handed the list across. "I believe that Maxim and Ivan Popov were out of the country at the time of your son's death, but I have not been able to find anything that ties the other two into the crime. My gut tells me they didn't do it but I wanted your opinion."

Borya passed the list back and shook his head. "None of these would cross me. None of them would do this. My son is a fool to give these names to you, he sends you on a, how you say, while duck chase."

"A wild goose chase, now that is interesting." Lola felt an exciting tingle raise the hairs on her arms. It happened when she got an inkling about who had committed the crime. Dare she push this with Borya?

"Spit it out," Borya said.

"When you are trying to solve a crime, the first thing to look at is who would benefit. There are two deaths here, that of your son and yours. Who would benefit from your death?"

"There is only one person, he said he was out of the country. I cannot go there, but you can. If he did this, find out how and stop him. Now, you must go I have work to do."

"Thank you," Lola said as she stood up. Sassy came trotting across as Lola walked out with Father Jackson.

"That was very unhelpful," Father Jackson said. "He almost said that he knew who did this but he wouldn't tell you."

"He told me," Lola said. "I just have to find a way to prove what he said."

WHAT NOW?

By the time Lola had dropped off Father Jackson, she was exhausted. There was still a team going through the shed at the churchyard, and they would not allow either Lola or the father to go near it.

A small crowd had grown around the church and Lola was worried about the father. He shrugged off her concerns. "Do not worry about me, I have God and justice on my side."

As Lola strapped Sassy into the Discovery to make the journey home, she could see the father giving a talk to the people there. She knew he would be telling them to avoid rumors and gossip and to wait for the full facts to come out. She also knew that he would defend Tony, despite what it may do to his own reputation.

Soon Lola was pulling up outside Tanya's house. The lights were on and she was so pleased to be back. Maybe she could find out some more tonight but she really needed to rest for a little while... and yet, with Tony locked up it felt wrong to rest.

"I tired too, and hungry," Sassy said.

Lola reached over and unclipped her harness and picked her up snuggling her close. The feel of her short soft coat made everything seem a little better. Sassy nuzzled up into Lola's hair and made strange little snuffly noises.

"Let's get you some food."

Sassy let out a bark of joy.

"Hi," Tanya called as Lola came in. "I picked up a take-away and we were just dishing up. You seem to have timed this perfectly." Tanya winked as Lola walked past.

"Sorry!" Lola laughed. "It's my turn to grab one at the weekend."

"I was only kidding," Tanya said. "Tikka Marsala good for you?"

"Great, thanks." Lola was already pouring some kibble into Sassy's bowl. The little Frenchie was trying to sit as she knew she had to but her bottom couldn't stay on the ground.

Lola held the dish up. "Mine, mine, mine, mine," was all Lola could hear. She chuckled as Sassy managed to stay still for a fraction of a second. Lola put the dish on the floor. Sassy leaned forward but caught herself. "Ohhhh!" And sat back down.

"Okay," Lola said and Sassy launched at the bowl. It was pink with a spiral of plastic inside to slow Sassy down as she tended to eat too quickly. When Lola had been recommended she doubted that the little dog would get her snub nose into the crevices but Sassy managed with no problem, using her tongue to scoop out the food if needed.

It slowed her down enough and she didn't seem to mind.

Wayne came down the stairs in a dark gray tracksuit with a towel on his head. "How's it going with Tony?" he asked.

As they ate the delicious curry, Lola explained all she knew and how she was at a bit of an impasse. Though she had a suspect he had an alibi, he was in Europe, in France at the time of the murder.

"Have you checked his alibi?" Wayne asked.

Lola hadn't but she got the feeling that he wouldn't have given it to them if it wasn't solid. "He offered it too quickly for me," Lola said.

"Well, he could prove this to the police by the stamps on his passport. Before Brexit, it would be hard to prove as there was free movement. Now it is much easier. There could, of course, be CCTV or hotel receipts, travel receipts, but now the passport would be considered incontrovertible." Wayne had that smile on his face he wore when he was hiding something.

"What is it?" Lola asked.

"Well, the suspects you have are all well connected to the underground world," Wayne said.

"You think he could have gone to France, booked into the hotel, and then was smuggled back into the country?" Lola asked.

"That is one way but I can think of an easier way. Have you never read Jason Bourne?"

Lola shook her head. "I don't understand."

Wayne chuckled. "If I was a Russian gangster I would probably have a fake passport as well as a real one. I go out of the country on the real one, come back on the fake, go back out on the fake, come home on the real."

Lola's head was spinning. "That makes sense. How could I find this out?"

"You would have to find the passport, which would not be easy. However, most crooks make silly mistakes. If your suspect does not think you are on to him he won't get rid of the passport. It will most likely be in some luggage."

"Near his socks perhaps!" Lola said without realizing she had said it out loud."

Tanya laughed. "I think you've had one too many gin's."

"Did I just say that out loud?"

"And I thought it was just Sassy who's obsessed with socks," Wayne said pouring a little more gin into Lola's glass. "Now, we find out that Lola has been training her to steal them all the time!"

Lola chuckled. "You got me." But it gave her an idea. "Could I borrow your passports?"

"Sure. But why?" Tanya said.

"Mine's still back at my place." Wayne shrugged. "It's just about the only thing that is."

The two of them chuckled and clinked glasses and Lola knew she had to get her own place sorted soon. There was still some more work to do on it but her friends deserved their privacy.

"I want to see if Sassy can find them. If a passport has a distinctive enough scent for her to be able to search for one."

"Great idea," Wayne said but the slight dent in his eyebrows showed Lola that he didn't have a lot of faith in her short-nosed sniffing dog.

She would prove him wrong. Sassy had a good length of nose for a Frenchie and she was incredibly good at finding things, especially socks.

Once the meal was finished Lola planned to return to her room to do some research and to see if Sassy could find her passport. Tanya ran upstairs to grab hers. As she opened the bedroom door Sassy ran inside and straight to her laundry basket in the en suite.

"Sassy!" Tanya yelled as the little Frenchie darted out of her room, a pair of trainer socks clasped firmly in her jaws.

Downstairs Lola and Wayne were chuckling. "I'll get them," Lola called.

"No need, they're Wayne's," Tanya said as she came back into the room with her passport.

Lola felt that tug of excitement. Tony may have to spend one night in jail but perhaps she now had a way to get him out. It would not be that easy but she had an idea, all be it a dangerous one. If she was right, she would have to go into the killer's home. Could she pull it off or would she end up in as many pieces as Alexander?

TRAINING

*L*ola sat on the floor of her bedroom with Sassy and a tub of small dog treats. Sassy was trained to both a clicker and a word. A device that made a distinctive sound to mark a correct behavior and a clicker word which in her case was "food."

This was part of her service dog training and it was very effective. The word or click could mark the exact time that she did something right and the sound or word would evoke a Pavlovian response. So named after the trainer who first used it, Pavlov, who found that if you gave a dog food after you rang a bell, eventually the dog would salivate at the sound of the bell without the food being present.

Lola, of course, did not need the word or clicker as she could communicate with Sassy. However, to Sassy Lola was slow and clumsy, and marking the precise moment with a clicker was much more effective.

Lola had hidden Tanya's passport at the side of her chest of drawers. She had made sure that she had walked all over the room so that Sassy couldn't track her footsteps to that spot. Now she sat on the floor with her own passport to see if it was a distinctive enough smell for the dog to be able to find.

"What this?" Sassy asked as Lola produced the passport.

"It's a passport."

"Looks like book, thin book," Sassy said.

"I want you to smell it and ignore my scent. Would you be able to recognize a different passport?"

Sassy sat down on her butt with her back legs stuck out, her head slumped forward a little and her bottom lip protruded. It was her normal stance when she was sulking or confused.

"If different not same so how I find?"

Lola could understand the little dog's point of view. The concept was difficult to describe. "Socks."

"Me likes socks." The lip had gone and her mouth was open in a smile. Her amber eyes were bright and her tongue hung out from her purple lips.

"I know you do, you must stop stealing them."

"Why?"

Lola knew this was too long a conversation for tonight. They were both tired and she wanted to go to the church in the morning before meeting Patricia. She also wanted to do some research tonight. She wanted to see if she could pull the accounts of a couple of the Russian businesses. It might lead to a motive.

"Okay, how do you tell something is socks as they are all different?"

The lip was out again. "Just can. Smelly so nice."

"Okay, let's try this." Lola reached out and scratched behind her ears. "Smell this and see what you can discern, ignore me."

Sassy took a great big sniff, pushing her snout into the passport and running it over the cover sniffing all the time. Lola knew she didn't need to do this, when she was tracking the scent just seemed to magically go up her nose and she could follow it at an amazing speed.

"What do you smell?"

"Paper, plastic, itty bits of metal, glue, dust, skin, eggs…"

"Wow, eggs?"

"You had eaten eggs when you touched this, it in grease in your skin."

Lola felt her jaw drop, it was months since she had touched her passport but Sassy was right, she had eaten an Egg Foo Yung that night.

"Okay, ignore the eggs. I imagine most passports will have all the rest but the dust and the skin will be different. I've hidden a different passport in this room, can you find it?"

Sassy looked at the treats and the clicker and then at Lola. If she couldn't talk to Sassy she would have clicked and treated her for taking the scent. Sassy was giving her a look to tell her that she was being tight with the treats.

"Sorry," Lola said and gave her one of the small cheese treats. "You get five if you find it."

Sassy's eyes widened and she jumped up and sniffed the air. "I have to search. I have to ignore that one." Her nose pointed at the passport in Lola's hands. Turning in a circle she sniffed the room. The look of disappointment on her face told Lola that the passport scent was not strong enough to penetrate this far, or that the passport she held in her own hands was blocking the scent.

Lola stood and took her passport out of the room. When she came back in Sassy was searching the edges of the room. She would search from left to right in a methodical manner. She was still taking in big exaggerated sniffs to prove that she was working.

Bit by bit she worked around the room until she came to the chest of drawers. Her tail, which had been wagging away as she worked, went stiff. She froze for a moment and then worked along the front of the drawers straight to where the passport was hidden. "I got it, cheesy."

Lola clicked and came over dropping some cheese treats as she recovered the passport. "You are so clever," she said, hugging Sassy close as she fed her a lot more than 5 cheesy treats.

"I know, like this game, hide it again!"

Lola laughed. "I'd love to but I have work to do." She put Sassy down.

"You boring," Sassy said and she sat looking so cute that Lola couldn't resist giving her an extra couple of treats.

It was good, Sassy could find a passport but how long would she need? Would they ever be in the right room to find it? Would it be safe to let her try?

With these questions running around her mind, Lola sat down at the computer and accessed Companies House. The British website held the accounts of all British companies. She had two to check and then she was done for the night. Somehow, she didn't think that sleep would come easy. She had let Tony down and her fear was that she wouldn't be able to find the real killer, or at least not before too much damage was done

A ROUGH NIGHT

"You let me down," the man's voice came out of the darkness. "It was your fault, you got to go home and left me here." A blood-covered hand reached out of the gloom.

"No, I'm sorry, I'm so sorry." Tears stung the back of Lola's eyes and trickled down her cheeks as she tried to reach out to her friend. Sweat was dripping down her brow and neck, it was gathering in her back. Her hands were moist and it made it hard to grip the rifle. "I tried."

"Not bad place."

Lola felt something warm and comforting touch her back and her mind was flooded with love. It didn't make sense, this place was dark and hot, the air so dry it was hard to breathe, it was the worst place ever.

Something scratched her arm. Something was patting her arm and she jerked awake. Sassy! Sassy had woken her from a nightmare. It was all a dream, just another dream. Niles would never have blamed her for what happened. The shame was in her own mind only.

Lola glanced at her watch, it was 6:30, she may as well get up. First, she rolled over and lifted Sassy up. Placing little kisses on the Frenchie's cheek. "Thank you, I don't know what I would do without you."

Sassy snuggled in close to her and mumbled back her own gratitude.

"Should we get up?" Lola asked.

Sassy curled up in the duvet and tucked her nose between her paws. "Sleep a little bit longer."

"You can, I'm going to do my stretches and have a shower."

"Stretches funny," Sassy said.

Lola knew what the little Frenchie meant. She couldn't understand why Lola had to do stretches in one go. In her mind, it made more sense to do them as she went about her day. So you got up and stretched while doing it. As she jumped out of the car she stretched before she walked away. Lola had tried to explain that it might not be acceptable for her to just go into a stretch as she went about her day. That people might laugh at her if she dropped to her knees and started doing the Downward Dog or the Superman stretch in the local shop.

The conversation had confused Sassy, she couldn't understand why people would find it funny. Lola had to admit that it would be so lovely to be a dog and to not have to worry about such things. Dogs were so accepting.

Leaving Sassy curled up on the bed, Lola began to do her stretches. She had received a few knocks and bumps during her time in the military and if she didn't exercise regularly, her body stiffened up. Most mornings, she liked to do 10 minutes before she jumped in the shower, just to keep things going. Sometimes, Sassy would get involved. After all, if Lola was on the floor then she must be there to cuddle Sassy.

It made it rather difficult to get into the Butterfly Fold or the Upward Dog when your own dog wanted to be underneath you. However, Lola had to admit it made it fun.

Once her stretches were done she went into the en suite to have a shower. Sassy was still curled up on the bed. Yesterday must've tired her out. They had been on the go a lot and then they had done the training on finding the passport. Though a dog used its nose instinctively, Lola had read that it could be quite tiring for them to learn such things.

Lola was dressed, and Sassy was just starting to get off the bed. To allow her to sneakily get Lola's bed socks, Lola went back into the en suite. She had to pretend that she wasn't aware of what Sassy was doing. It was part of the game and stealing Lola's socks was no fun if she knew about it.

Humming to herself, Lola walked into the en suite and pretended to be tidying her hair. The long black locks seemed to have a life of their own. They should've been so easy to look after and yet Lola was never able to keep them where she wanted them. Removing the bungee, she put a comb through her hair and quickly fastened it back up. That should be long enough.

Sneakily moving to the door, she peeked around the frame. Sure enough, Sassy was on the bed. The little dog checked that no one was looking and then dived on Lola's bed socks.

Lola suffered from cold feet, no matter what the weather. So she always wore bed socks when she first went to bed. However, halfway through the night, her feet would get too hot and so she would take them off and put them next to her pillow. For some reason, these socks were Sassy's favorite, and every morning she had to pinch them.

Sassy dived on the socks, picked them up, and tossed them into the air. She turned quickly and grabbed them as they fell. One more quick look around and she jumped off the bed, threw the socks up once more, and when they landed, she rolled on them.

Lola was trying desperately not to chuckle and give away the game that she was watching. On the floor, Sassy was rolling on the socks for all she was worth. Lola could take it no more. This was so cute and so funny that she let out a chuckle and came out of the en suite.

"What are you doing?" Lola asked.

Sassy gave one more good roll, jumped up, picked the socks up, and dived under a chair. Then she peered out at Lola with the socks held under her paws. "Rolling on sockys I get smelley's all over me, so when I go hunting, squirrels think I'm you."

Sassy looked so pleased with this that Lola didn't have the heart to tell her that the squirrels would run away from her just as much as they would Sassy.

"Can I keep sockys?" Sassy asked.

Lola didn't have the heart to take them off her and they needed to go in the wash anyway, so she nodded. "We have a busy day again today, are you up for it?"

"Me ready."

Lola really hoped that today would be a better day and that they could get Tony out of jail. If only he would use his alibi, then maybe this would be over. However, that wasn't certain. Daniel Peterson might believe that Maureen Cooper was lying to save Tony. It was ludicrous, that she would destroy her husband's career for that, but that doubt might be enough to keep Tony in jail.

Lola's stomach rolled as she worried that she would not be capable of doing this. The last thing she needed was to let someone down, again.

Quickly, she pushed the thought away before it tore down her confidence. Logically, she knew she had nothing to feel guilty about. What happened in Afghanistan was not her fault. There was nothing she or anyone else could have done about it. She knew it was survivor's guilt, she knew she had to let it go — if only she could.

Maybe, if she got Tony off, then that would be a start. But how, how could she do this?

BETTY'S

*L*ater that morning, Lola picked Father Jackson up and drove him into Lincoln to see Patricia. They were meeting at Betty's Tea Room. It was a beautiful old building, dating from the 1600s, the Tudor period. The bottom half was brick while the top half was white with black timber.

As they climbed Steep Hill on the way, Sassy began to spin in circles and dance about.

"Flying cake place," she said, yipping with joy.

"Is she all right?" Father Jackson asked.

"I use Betty's for some of my client meetings. There was one where a lady talked with her hands... while holding her food."

"Oh, my," he said.

"Sassy remembers the place; if she could talk, she would call it Flying Food Café. She gets very excited when we come here.

"If... I talk good!" Sassy huffed and trotted off up the hill while the two humans were panting and struggling a little on the steep climb.

"I've always wondered about this hill," Lola said.

"What do you mean?" Father Jackson asked.

"Well, I hate to say this but the land for miles and miles around is flat, and yet here is this beautiful city built on a hill that seems to come out of nowhere? Was it manmade?"

"Oh, no, not at all. The Lincoln Edge as it is called, I believe was formed out of resistant Jurassic Limestone but Alice would know more than me."

"It gives the city such a strategic position," she said, her military mind kicking in.

"Of course," Father Jackson said. "I'm sure it's why it was built here and the Romans used Lincoln as one of their main towns for many years, settling here in AD50. There are still many Roman roads throughout the county. It was originally called Lindon. The fortress at the top of the hill was then used for retiring soldiers as a Colonia. Lindon became Lindum Colonia and eventually Lincoln."

"That is fascinating. Is it just at Lincoln? The Edge I mean?"

Father Jackson laughed. "No, It runs for 50 miles from Grantham to the Humber and is 50 meters high."

They made it to the top. The café was nestled in a square just before Lincoln's cathedral to the right and the castle to the left. The square was always busy and today it was buzzing with people, both local and tourists. Lola had still not visited either of these magnificent attractions, but she would one day.

As always there was a queue to go into Betty's Tearoom and Gerald Munro ably managed that line. Dressed as a butler, the tall impressive man appeared to look down on all that crossed his path. However, as he saw Lola, Sassy, and Father Jackson he called to them.

"Miss Ramsay, Miss Darnell is waiting for you, please come through."

"Thank you, Gerald," Lola said as a waitress guided them through the busy cafe to a secluded table.

Betty's was like stepping back in time. Pristine white table cloths covered round tables that were set with fine bone china tea sets in an amazing array of colors. The conversation buzzed and cutlery clinked as people enjoyed a little escape and good food. Most tables had a fine-bone china cake stand piled high with delicious fare.

The waitress weaved them through the tables. Lola felt Sassy pull on her lead, she darted beneath a table and gobbled down a morsel of something that had been dropped there. The smile on her face said that she wasn't worried that it had been on the floor. Maybe it wasn't that nice to be a dog, after all. Lola certainly preferred her cakes to stay on the plate.

They arrived at a corner table, secluded in an alcove. Patricia stood and shook their hands. "Sit. I ordered a pot of tea for three and an afternoon tea for us all. I thought that way we could eat and talk and see where we go from here."

"Lovely," Father Jackson said taking a seat.

Lola nodded and sat down, she wanted to ask if Tony was free but she knew he wasn't.

"Did you manage to get Tony released?" Father Jackson asked beating Lola to it.

"I'm sorry but that wasn't possible. I have spoken to him this morning and he is in good spirits. He just keeps asking about the dog. I assured him he is fine."

"I will get Alice to send you some more pictures," Lola said. "When you see him you can show him them."

"That would be good. We must keep his spirits up at this time. Now, let me tell you what I have found out." Patricia opened a file on the table and turned to the first page.

It was a list of some sort but Lola couldn't read it from where she was.

The tea arrived before they could go any further and Father Jackson poured them all a cup. Lola took hers black, and they all grabbed a sandwich off the platter before them.

"There is some quite incriminating evidence that needs explaining," Patricia began.

"Before we go any further, have you had any more thoughts about Tony giving the police his alibi?" Lola asked.

Father Jackson sucked in a breath.

Patricia shook her head. "He is not prepared to do so at the moment. The election is a month away and... well." Patricia shook her head and took a sip of tea. Lola got the feeling that she was doing this to give herself time to think. "Well, by that time it would seem that he had somehow manufactured his alibi. I believe that if he doesn't use it now, then it will not make a good defense."

"Oh!" Lola said.

"Make food fly, boring," Sassy said and pawed at Lola's leg.

Lola knew that she couldn't very well tell the Frenchie that these people would not be throwing food at her and so she had to keep quiet. Surreptitiously, she snuck a little bit of sandwich down to her.

Patricia seemed very efficient but she wondered if it would be enough to get Tony off. For the first time since this began she wondered if he would spend the rest of his life in jail.

HAVE YOUR CAKE AND EAT IT

Sassy pawed Lola's leg. "Don't be sad, you can eat all of cake, I not hungry."

Lola smiled and passed her down another piece of sandwich. It filled her with hope, that the little dog was prepared to give up the sweet treats to make her feel better. In a world with that much love, surely, justice had to prevail.

As they picked at the sandwiches, Patricia told them what she had found out. It was not a pretty picture.

"The police have what they consider incriminating evidence," Patricia said. "I know you have seen the photos that were plastered on the walls of the back room. They led the police to believe that Tony was obsessed with Alexander and that he had been tracking him for some time."

"No, no," Father Jackson said shaking his head and putting down his cup with quite a clank. "Tony wouldn't do that. Apart from which, he wouldn't have had time."

Patricia held up her hand. "I am not agreeing with this, I am just stating the fa... the evidence that the police have. Once we have everything out in the open, then we can discuss how it got there." Taking a few moments, she locked her eyes with Father Jackson. Willing him to understand that she was on their side.

The priest nodded and lowered his head. "I apologize, continue."

"They found other things in the back room, some of which they are still working on but what they have released to me is that they found a Bible that belongs to yourself, Father Jackson, and has your fingerprints on it. And they found a workbook that belonged to Tony, and has his fingerprints on it."

"These went missing a few weeks ago, I told you, Lola, I asked you if you could find them if you remember?"

"Yes, I do remember and it was before the body was found." Lola knew that it didn't matter when he had told her or what she said. Daniel Peterson was never going to believe it.

"They found two mobile phones as well, but they hadn't processed them last I spoke. Have you lost any phones?" Patricia asked.

Father Peterson shook his head. "No, I have to use a mobile, I couldn't run the parish without it, but it's not something I like to use or am that comfortable with. I certainly wouldn't have a second one or two."

"Well, that is quite worrying," Patricia said. "They were obviously put in that room for a reason."

"Is that all the evidence they have?" Lola asked.

"It's enough, but they have a few other bits and pieces. A monograph handkerchief with Alexander's blood on. And then there is the autopsy report which we will go through too."

"Does the autopsy say anything that can help us?" Lola asked.

"Ooohhh, cake," Sassy said in Lola's mind. Lola looked in the direction of the Frenchie's gaze to see that a piece of cake had just landed on the floor. The people at the table hadn't noticed and they weren't far away. Before

Lola could stop her, Sassy had tugged the lead out of her hand and trotted over to fetch it.

"I won't go into too many details of the autopsy, not while we're eating," Patricia said. "The main take-away is that it could not have been something like Tony's ax that caused the injuries. I know that the police are still checking the tools at the churchyard, however, the cuts were very clean. Not exactly surgi-cal, but I would say... well, mechanical, almost like a guillotine."

"So, we are looking for a heavy industrial cutter of some form?" Lola asked.

"Yes, I would think so," Patricia said. "I would imagine the sort of thing that you would find in a factory."

"So, if you can find that," Father Jackson said his face alive with hope, "after all this time, will they still find evidence on it?"

"I'd be able to sniff blood," Sassy said, to let Lola know that she was listening to the conversation.

Lola passed her down a piece of cake as a thank you. She may need to take her up on that.

"What were the initials on the handkerchief?" Father Jackson asked and his face had turned almost as white as the tablecloth.

Patricia quickly checked her file. "It was P J," she said.

"Oh my, oh my, this is bad," Father Jackson said as he reached into his pocket and pulled out a handkerchief. The initials on it were P and J. "My name is Peter Jackson. My mother bought me these many many years ago. Very few people use handkerchiefs never mind about monographed ones. This can only be to smear my name too."

"I cannot deny that this is bad news," Patricia said. "Is there any way that someone could have come across one of your handkerchiefs?"

"I don't know." he said.

Lola had noticed that Sassy was leaning against him and Father Jackson had reached down to stroke her without even noticing it.

"Who does your washing?" Lola asked.

"Since my wife passed, I do it myself," he said.

"And where do you dry your washing?" Lola asked.

The father's eyes widened as he understood and he nodded his head. "Of course, I dry it on the washing line at the bottom of my garden. It is close to the churchyard. Anyone could have taken one of my handkerchiefs and I would be none the wiser."

"What do we do about this?" Lola asked.

"It will not take the police long to find out, I will go see them after this meeting. If it is not already too late."

Oh no, Lola could not believe this was happening. Who could be evil enough to not only frame Tony but to frame Father Jackson too?

MORE BAD NEWS

The atmosphere at the table was charged. Patricia no doubt wanted to get back and see what the police knew. Father Jackson was terrified that his career, possibly even his life as he knew it was over. Lola felt that she must be to blame for all of this. If only she was a better investigator, then she would've found some evidence to exonerate her friends.

"You good, tell me what sniffys were in that place and I'll tell you who did it," Sassy said.

Something about what she had said forged an idea in Lola's mind. "You said that the diary and the Bible had fingerprints on them?" Lola asked.

"Yes, I did," Patricia said.

"I presume that they did a full forensic sweep of the room at the back of the shed. Did they find DNA and fingerprints anywhere else in that room?"

Lola noticed the change in Patricia's face, even though she did her best to hide it. She was excited. Quickly, she scanned through the folder that she had received from the police. Reading a note here, checking a column there. "No, they didn't."

"I don't understand what you're saying." Father Jackson said.

Lola and Patricia shared a glance and Patricia raised her hand to indicate that Lola should be the one to tell him the good news.

"If either yourself or Tony had been in that back room, there would be DNA or fingerprint evidence to prove it. The fact that the only fingerprints were on two items in the room makes it highly unlikely that you were the ones who placed the other items there. It is illogical and would be almost impossible unless you were to wear gloves and a forensic suit all the time you were in that room... and if you did, then why would you leave fingerprints on two items?"

Father Jackson was grinning. "Then we can get Tony off!"

Patricia shook her head. "I wish we could, however, a lack of evidence does not prove innocence. Don't get me wrong, at a trial, the jury would find it very hard to ignore and it would certainly introduce doubt, definitely reasonable doubt. That does not mean that a man like Daniel Peterson wouldn't still take this to court."

"What would that mean for Tony?" Father Jackson asked.

"I hate to say this," Patricia said, "his life would be destroyed even if he was found innocent."

"Then we have to prove that he didn't do this," Father Jackson said.

Patricia and Lola both agreed with him. Lola didn't like to say that they had to prove that he was innocent too. Once Daniel Peterson found out that the handkerchief was his and whatever he found on the phones then she knew they would be coming for the father. Could she find a way to exonerate him first?

It took just another half an hour for Patricia to fill them in on everything she had found. There was nothing that Lola thought would be useful, nothing that she thought she could investigate further.

Patricia promised them that she would keep them informed and left. Lola finished her tea and handed a couple more pieces of cake down to Sassy. The father seemed too preoccupied to eat anything and she was worried about him.

"Let me take you home," Lola said.

"Thank you, I need to pray on this. I have to find a way to help Tony for he does not deserve any of this."

"I couldn't agree more," Lola told him.

As they walked back down Steep Hill, weaving in and out of the people on their way up, Lola felt a little bit lost. Every one of these people thought that their life would carry on the way it was. None of them expected that tomorrow they may be in jail, or gone, suddenly, she felt as if life was all too short.

"Why sad?" Sassy said in her mind.

Lola scooped her up so she could whisper into her ear and not have the father think that she was going crazy. "Friends of mine are in trouble."

"My friends too, I want to help," Sassy said.

Suddenly, Lola had an idea. Maybe Sassy could help.

"Father Jackson, are the police still looking at the shed? Is it still a crime scene?"

"No, they finished off early this morning. They have all gone and they have removed the tape and told me that I can go back in whenever I want. They didn't help me put everything back which I'm rather disappointed at. They left it scattered all over the graveyard and I really do have to get it tidied up. It is disrespectful for people visiting their loved ones, it is an eyesore."

"I can help with that and I'm sure I can find a few other people to help too," Lola said. "But first, I want to have a look in the shed and take Sassy in with me. Can I ask, have you been in the back room since this happened?"

"No, I haven't been in it for years."

"Good, I have a plan," Lola said.

SNIFFYS

Once Lola had dropped the father back at the church, she dropped her car back at Tanya's house to find Wayne was there.

"How are things going?" he asked.

Lola quickly filled him in on what had been going on and the lack of evidence on one hand and the excessive of evidence on the other.

"It definitely sounds like a frame job. Part of me wishes I was on the case, but part of me is glad I'm not. However, I wish it was anyone other than Danny Boy. What are your plans now?"

Lola explained what she was going to do. "Then, I might end up helping Father Jackson put all the things back into the shed. I was going to call Sam and see if he would help for a little bit of pocket money."

"I'm sure he would be glad to help, why don't I come and help too? I have the afternoon off and who knows, I might be useful."

"That would be great," Lola said. Wayne was an impressive and strong-looking man. He would make short work of clearing up the churchyard.

"I'll be down in about half an hour," Wayne said.

"I'll walk down," Lola said, "it's hardly worth taking the car."

Sassy was spinning around in circles having heard one of her favorite words, walk.

"Come on then, let's get you a harness on," Lola said and reached down. Sassy leaped into her arms ready for the harness to be strapped onto her.

As they made the short walk to the church Lola explained what she wanted. "Can you remember what Tony smells like?"

"Yes."

"Can you remember what Father Jackson smells like?"

"Of course, he smells of ginger biscuits."

Lola chuckled. "He's very lucky. When we get into the back of the shed I want you to tell me if either Tony or Father Jackson have been there, can you do that?"

"Yes, I sniffy sniffs good good." Sassy seemed to be strutting down the street now, she was proud to be trusted with this task.

While they finished the walk, Lola dialed Sam Smith, a young man who helped her out on occasion. The first time she had met him he had been going down the wrong path but with Sassy's help, he had turned around and was now studying to be a policeman. From time to time, he helped her out with a little bit of surveillance or other jobs that she needed.

"Hi, Sam, how are you doing?" Lola asked.

"I'm so pleased you called, I wanted to see you, maybe tomorrow?" Sam said and there was something in his voice that made her worried.

"Are you okay?" Lola asked.

"It's about my mum, and Brent, I think she's seeing him again and I'm worried."

Lola had not expected this. Brent Burton was a rich businessman and quite a predator. Lola believed that he was Sam's father and that his mother had been underage, however, Rebecca, or Becky, was not prepared to say anything. The last thing Sam needed was for the two of them to be back together.

Becky Smith was a good woman. She had worked hard to see that Sam had a roof over his head, good food, and clean clothes to wear. Lola liked her but she just wished that she didn't have such a soft spot for Brent.

"Sam, I wish I could help but I can't see you tomorrow, or at least I don't think I can." Lola quickly explained about Tony and Father Jackson. She didn't mind telling Sam as his loyalty was assured and she may need to ask for his help at some time. Luckily, he understood that she couldn't see him straight away but he asked that she do so as soon as she could. Lola told him to ring her when he was free; if she could meet, she would; if not, she assured him she would see him as soon as she had the time. Unfortunately, he was not free to help out.

"You more sad," Sassy said. "I wish I had socks, that would make you happy."

"You have plenty of socks," Lola said.

"Not got any with me." Sassy stopped and turned around, her eyes were open wide and she was looking down at Lola's feet. "You wearing socks, take them off give them to me I give them back, you be happy."

Lola chuckled. "Then my feet will be cold."

"See, it made you happy. Socks are just the best."

Lola had to admit it, she was chuckling, but they were here now so it was time to be serious.

Lola took Sassy into the shed. "Tony and Father Jackson have been in this part can you smell them?"

Sassy stopped before taking her exaggerated sniffs. "Tony here, Tony here... Father Jackson here... both here... micey's here."

Before Sassy could go over every inch of the shed, Lola stopped her. "That's great. Now, we're going to go into the back room and see if you can tell me if they've been in there."

Lola had a bag in her pocket as she always did and she used that to open the door. She knew it was silly, the scene had already been processed, but she didn't want to remove any evidence or add anything of her own to the scene. The door was stiff but she noticed that the hinges had been oiled. Had the police done that? Or was it done before?

"Sassy, can you tell how new this oil is?" Lola pointed at the hinges.

Sassy took in a great big sniff and then coughed and spluttered. "Horrid. But very old. Older than Sassy herself."

Lola got the feeling that the little dog had not quite understood what she meant. This happened sometimes and she knew it would be too difficult to explain the principles. The oil was old, how long it had been there was a different matter.

"Thank you."

Lola pulled the door open and unclipped Sassy's lead. "I'm going to stay here, so I won't contaminate the scene. It will make it easier for you to sniff out who has been there."

Sassy walked in sniffing high and low in great big exaggerated snuffles. "Lots of people been in here, same as in other room." Sassy was looking back and grinning.

"Well done, can you smell Tony or Father Jackson?"

Sassy started walking around the room from the left-hand side. "Not here," she drew in a great big sniff and walked a few more steps. "Not here." She walked a little further and sniffed again on the ground to her left, to her right up in the air. "Not here."

Lola wanted to chuckle but she mustn't. The little Frenchie went all the way around the room sniffing almost every inch and everywhere she went she said, "not here."

"Do you recognize anyone else who has been in the room?"

"Nasty man from police has been everywhere," Sassy said as she took in a few more sniffs. "PC Jenkins, others I do not know. But..., there is someone I met but can't remember. If I sniffy him again I know him."

Lola felt the excitement growing inside of her. The hairs raised on her arms. Now she knew that Tony had definitely been framed. If he had never been in the back room then no way could he have done any of this. Of course, she couldn't prove that but it gave her an idea. She was pretty sure she knew who had killed Alexander Petrov, the only problem was, how could she prove it?

TROUBLE FOR THE FATHER

*L*ola was in a quandary. She had promised Father Jackson that she would help him load everything back into the shed, but she didn't want to just yet. She may need to let Sassy go back in there and take the scent again.

She decided to ask him if he would leave it all for a while and was wandering over to his house when the sound of police sirens broke the peace. It set her nerves racing and rose the hairs on her arms. Of course, it could be anything but somehow she knew it was bad news.

"Not bad place," Sassy said but even she didn't seem as sure as usual.

"I know, sweetie, I think it's bad people."

"I bite them," Sassy growled and shook her head as if she was attacking Peterson's trousers once more.

"Promise me you won't do that," Lola said.

"Ok!"

Sassy seemed a little subdued. Maybe it was because of how much Lola had been stressed these last few days. Maybe she should try to be more cheerful. However, the last thing Lola wanted was for the spiteful officer to invoke the Dangerous Dogs Act on her little friend.

Before Lola could get to Father Jackson's door, two marked police cars screeched to a stop on the street outside. 4 uniformed officers and Daniel Peterson piled out of the cars and ran up to the father's house.

They hammered on his door. "Police, open up, police!"

Lola stepped back so she was out of their line of sight and watched.

Father Jackson opened the door and she stepped out so he could see her. He nodded and then looked back at the officers.

"We have a warrant for your arrest," Daniel said. "I am arresting you under suspicion of the murder of Alexander Petrov. You do not have to say anything.

But, it may harm your defense if you do not mention when questioned something which you later rely on in court."

Lola watched as they put handcuffs on the father and took him to the cars and then he was gone. A feeling of guilt, shame, and anger washed over her. How had she let this happen?

"Not your fault," Sassy said as she pawed Lola's leg.

"I know, sweetie."

Lola rang Patricia and explained what had happened. It was a relief that the solicitor was calm, and confident that she could get the father out. She promised Lola that she would call her soon.

"I have a theory," Lola said. "I don't want to explain it just yet, in case I tip the person off, but I am working on this."

"Well, any help you can give would be greatly received!" Patricia said.

"Do you know why they arrested Father Jackson?"

Patricia was silent for a moment and Lola thought she had already gone. "No, but I suspect it has something to do with the phones. They were there for a reason."

"Do you believe that they were framed?" Lola asked.

"It is not my job to judge... however, I do. This evidence is too bitty. It is either solid or there is none at all, it doesn't make sense."

"This might not make much sense either but trust me it is true. My dog is trained to search for people, she couldn't find any trace of Father Jackson or Tony in the back room. I know this can't be evidence but I wanted you to know."

"If only she could talk to you and tell you who had been in there," Patricia said.

"I'm working on it," Lola replied before she said her goodbyes and hung up.

Now, she had to take a chance. Would it pay off or would she end up in danger?

When Lola had done her research, she had found out that Uri Petrov had a large industrial cutter in his workshop. It was used for slicing up cardboard and after a bit of research she had found out that it would be just as useful for chopping off a foot! That meant there were two of the Russians that had an industrial cutter that could have been used to commit the murder, as Maxim and Ivan Popov had a similar piece of equipment.

Uri was also deep in debt; with his brother gone and his father dying he would inherit a fortune.

It seemed that those who had both the motive and the ability to do this were out of the country at the time of the murder. All three of her suspects were in Europe.

Lola had decided to go and visit Uri Petrov at his home. Her excuse was to tell him that she was looking into Maxim and Ivan and that she needed his advice. She hoped that his arrogance and male ego would make him want to help her. However, it was not something she was looking forward to. Uri was dangerous and if she made a wrong move she could be in trouble.

Lola was making the short walk back to Tanya's. Going over and over her plan in her mind. She was miles away and didn't see Roy Patterdale until she was almost on top of him.

Lola jumped as Roy banged a placard onto the pavement and stepped out in front of her.

She shot backward and raised her arms to defend herself and Sassy barked furiously at the man before Lola realized that he was simply protesting about his hedges. "It's okay, Sassy."

The placard had the words Save our Hedges written on it. Roy waved it in front of Lola and stopped her in her tracks.

Sassy was now leaning against her, which stopped Lola from going into one of her attacks. Not six months ago, if somebody had done this, she would be curled up on the floor and whimpering. Now, all that had happened was that her heartbeat increased and she had readied herself for action.

"Would you sign my petition?" Roy asked and from somewhere he pulled out a clipboard and shoved it in front of her face.

"What is it for?" Lola asked a little bit foolishly. She had already spoken to him about the hedges and he was holding a placard to save them. It was obvious that the petition was to save the beautiful hedges from being cut back.

Roy sagged a little and leaned his placard against the hedge. "I'm calling on the Council to let me trim the hedges back a little bit each year," Roy said.

"I'm happy to sign." Lola took the offered pen from him and the clipboard. Roy turned around and offered his back which Lola leaned against. She squiggled her signature on it and then handed him the clipboard back. "Would it be so bad if they did trim them for you?"

"If they just trimmed them, and did it gradually, no, but they wouldn't. You see, they want to take over a foot and a half off the hedge. That would devastate it. Here let me show you." Taking hold of the hedge, he pulled the tightly knitted greenery apart and showed her that less than 6 inches inside the hedge there were simply bare branches.

Lola felt really sorry for him. If they cut the hedges back to that, it would look horrendous and there really was no need. The path was walkable on and the road was so quiet, what was the Council thinking?

"You really think they'll make you cut it?" Lola asked.

"I hope not, I have never been so angry about anything in my life and I really don't know what I will do. I guess I can sit here all day. Put myself in front of the clippers, but there's only one of me. If I find out who did this, who reported me..." A look of such fury crossed his face that Lola took a step back. "I don't know what I will do but it will not be very nice."

Sassy was leaning against Roy's leg. "Oh, aren't you the cutest little thing," Roy said and leaned down to stroke her.

"Do you know where this all came from?" Lola asked.

"Oh, do I ever." Roy was shaking his head now and his usually calm face was red, his fists clenched tightly around the clipboard whitening his knuckles. "I believe it was Lucinda Clinton-West. It was raised at the last village meeting. I didn't go, that will serve me right, I won't miss one again... and if... if she is the cause of the destruction of these hedges... Lord help me!"

"Village meeting?" Lola asked.

"Yes, we have them every 6 months. Village issues are raised and the councilor comes. They did a really good job with the phone lines last year. I just missed this one because I was away. I should have known it was Lucinda, she's always into everyone else's business. Such as, what is Jake doing with his field? The village should complain about Clarissa wanting to build an extension so her mother can move in, all that sort of thing. The woman's a menace."

"Oh, I will come to the next meeting, if I'm allowed," Lola said a little unsure what he wanted from her. Maybe it was just an ear to bend.

"You are sensible, you would be very welcome. Oh, if that woman destroys my hedges I don't know what I would do." His fists were clenched in front of him and there was a wild look in his eyes.

"I'm really sorry, Roy, but I do have to go. I hope that they don't force this on you and if I can be of any help please let me know."

"Of course. I will be here, I will defend these hedges with my life."

Lola smiled at him and walked on, she had once thought that this was a quiet and peaceful little village. At times, it seemed more hectic than a big city.

A buzzing drew her attention to her pocket and her phone began to ring. It was Sam. Lola answered. "Hi, Sam, how are you?"

"I need to see you, and I need to see you now," Sam said and she could tell that he was close to tears. This was not like him, he was a strong character and had been through so much. What could have made him feel like this?

"Is it really urgent?" Lola asked. Though Sam had never asked her for anything and she would do anything for him, right now she had other priorities.

"It is, please, I'm at the Lakeside Garden Center, can you meet me there?"

Lola wanted to say no but there was something about the young man's voice that told her she had to make the time. "I'll be there in 15 minutes."

HISTORY REPEATS ITSELF

*L*ola pulled into the garden center, her stomach grumbled and she realized that it was lunchtime and she had skipped breakfast. It wouldn't hurt to grab a bite to eat while she was here and the cafe was just amazing.

Behind the garden center was a field which was often full of geese and ducks. It was where Lola had parked and as they walked across it, Sassy's nose was glued to the grass.

"Birdy smellies, delicious and lots of poop. Can we stay out here for a bit?" Sassy asked.

"We have to meet Sam, he might be in trouble."

Sassy's body stiffened as she saw a blackbird land in front of them. A whine escaped her and the bird lifted on the wing and was gone. "Missed it, see Sam now."

Soon they had walked through the garden center and to the café around the back. It had seats inside where dogs weren't allowed but they were allowed at the outside seats which were next to a lake. As always, the place was reasonably busy and Lola with Sassy wandered through the crowded seating area until they saw Sam. It had been a long time since she had seen him looking so miserable. When she first met him he was running with a bad crowd and being bullied into behaving badly. Now, he had turned his life around, and he was usually a happy young man.

Sam spotted her and waved her over. "Thank you for coming," he said as they reached the secluded table.

"It's okay, I realized I haven't eaten. Would you like some lunch?"

Sam had already picked Sassy up and was cuddling her on his knee. "Thanks, that would be good."

That was not his normal enthusiastic answer, something was definitely wrong. "Would you like the special?" Lola asked.

Sam nodded. "And a cappuccino if I can have one please."

"Of course, look after Sassy, I won't be a minute."

Lola quickly went inside and ordered the food. The special today was a steak pie with roast potatoes, mashed potatoes, and vegetables, or with chips as the English called French fries. Lola ordered one with potatoes and one with chips, a pot of tea for herself, and the cappuccino for Sam. She returned to the table while they waited for the food.

"Now, tell me what is wrong," Lola asked.

Sam looked down at his hands and fiddled with his phone. "It's my mum, I think she's seeing Brent again, this morning she came home from work looking like this." Sam passed his phone across to Lola. "She said it was an accident but I know she went out last night before her shift this morning"

Lola sucked in a deep breath. Becky Smith had a terrible black eye. Had Brent really hit her? If he had, what could Lola do about it?

"We have to get your mum to testify," Lola said. "I checked English law and there is no statute of limitations. A simple blood test could end all of this and put

272

that awful man away where he belongs."

"The thing is, she says she loves him. It drives me crazy and I don't know what to do to keep her safe. Maybe I should go and have a word with him myself." Sam was wringing his hands together and Lola could see that he had been chewing his nails. She had to help him.

"I don't think that's a good idea. You must not put your career in danger, don't throw it all away just for a few weeks." Lola said but what could she do. Brent Burton was a very rich and influential man and most likely Sam's father. He was also a ladies' man and a bully.

Lola had helped another girl get away from him, and maybe she would testify, however, she had been older than Becky Smith was when he first dated her. Becky was barely 16 when she had Sam, how young she was when the relationship started, Lola dreaded to think.

Dated was not really the word she would use. Louisa Meek had been Brent's secretary, he had pressured her into a relationship. It made her miserable, but she had escaped and was now a happy and successful artist.

What could Lola do? She pulled out her phone and dialed Wayne.

"Hello, trouble," he said.

"Very funny, where did that come from?" Lola chuckled.

"It just came to me this moment, it seems to suit you. Now, what can I do for you?"

Lola quickly explained the situation with Becky Smith. How they believed that Sam was Brent Burton's son and that Becky had been underage when she became pregnant. She then explained about the blackeye and that Brent seemed to have some hold on Becky and asked what he could do.

Wayne was quiet for a moment. "Like I said, hello, trouble. It's a difficult one but if you give me her address I will go and talk to her."

Lola asked Sam if he liked that idea and he nodded.

Lola passed the address over to Wayne. "Before you go, did anyone look at Uri Petrov's financials? I had a quick look and his business is struggling but I couldn't look at his personal financials."

"You want to get me fired?" Wayne said with a chuckle. "If Danny Boy finds out I've been looking at his case he will throw his teddy out of the pram and cause a right ruckus."

"I'm sorry, I shouldn't have asked."

"It's okay, I like causing trouble," Wayne said and Lola could hear that he was tapping on his keyboard. "Here we go, Uri is in a lot of debt. Over a million pounds worth. Do you like him for this?"

"He is on my radar. I'm going to see him now, good luck with Becky."

Lola put the phone down just as their food arrived. For the first time today, she noticed that Sam's eyes lit up. It looked like his appetite was back now that he hoped his mother's problem would be solved. Lola didn't like to tell him that it wouldn't be this easy. Wayne could go and talk to her, but she could refuse to press charges. Not only could she refuse, Lola thought it was more than likely that she would.

The problem was not over yet, it was only just beginning. Lola hoped that Becky and Sam would stay safe and that she could persuade her to testify. Sam deserved so much more than Brent. Unfortunately, life is not always fair, but if he couldn't have the father he deserved, at least she hoped that the one he had would not be allowed to destroy his life.

"Me me me me me, hungry!" Lola heard in her mind and looked down to see that Sassy was sitting looking at her with the most adoring little face that she could muster.

Chuckling, Lola blew on a piece of chip and passed it down to her little furry friend.

THE LION'S DEN

When Lola left Sam at the garden center he was looking much happier. The radio was playing in her car and the news came on. Lola almost slammed on the brakes. "Oh no, this can't be happening."

The news was reporting that Father Jackson had been arrested for murder and that the parish had disavowed him. "If only I had been quicker," Lola said.

"Not your fault, you been busy, too busy to give me lots of treats and cuddles."

"I promise I'll make up for it when this case is over," Lola said. The news report finished and the music was playing but it did not bring her any peace. She turned the radio off and knew that no matter what the danger, she had to find the killer. She had known it would hit the news about Father Jackson but it had hit so quickly and already the parish had got rid of him. What was wrong with people? Whatever happened to innocent until proven guilty? Nowadays it seemed to be guilty as soon as the news ran the story, and the only thing the news was interested in was headlines. The truth was cast aside if a lie would make a better story, or at least it seemed that way.

Uri Petrov's apartment was in a rather new building looking out over the Bradford wharf, which was England's oldest inland harbor.

There was a multistory car park not far from there. Lola left the car there and with Sassy, she walked along the waterfront to the building. It was a beautiful place with the harbor on one side with a wide block paved walkway, lined on the other with restaurants and eateries. Maybe she should bring Tanya and Wayne for a meal here one night. It would be charming to sit outside with the lights on the water and all the boats across the way twinkling in the darkness.

The walk calmed her but she was nearly at the building she was looking for. It was called One the Brayford.

Would Uri see her? She hoped so.

Lola stood before the impressive-looking building. Her finger poised above the intercom button. What could she say? Then it came to her and she pressed the buzzer.

"Who is it?"

"Mr. Petrov, it's Lola Ramsay, we spoke some days ago. Your father asked me to look into the death of your brother and I could do with your help on those names you gave me. I believe it could be one of them, but I've hit a bit of a dead-end. Could I come up and talk to you?"

"Yes, come up. I'm on the top floor, turn right out of the elevator, I'm the penthouse apartment just in front of you."

The door buzzed letting Lola know that it was open. "Here we go," she said to Sassy. "Can you remember what the passport smelt like last night?"

"I remember."

"I want you to see if you can find the same smell in this man's apartment. You might have to sneak around a little and it may smell the same and yet different. Can you do that for me?"

"I sniffy out good," Sassy said and she seemed to square her shoulders and raise her head a little bit with pride. As they walked in Lola was sure that she was strutting her little Frenchie stuff. Sassy loved to feel useful.

"Just do it very carefully, he is a bad man and I don't want him to know what you're up to."

"I sneaky as a squirrel," Sassy said.

"I think it's sneaky as a Fox," Lola said as they entered the elevator.

"Squirrel so sneaky it blamed the Fox."

The elevator was soon on the top floor and the doors opened. The building was beautiful inside; champagne-colored walls with gold coving and a thick lush gold carpet, with intricate brown squares on it. The whole thing smelled of luxury and yet if Uri's financials were as bad as she believed, and this building was only a few years old, how could he afford it?

The door in front of her looked to be solid oak. Lola knocked and took in a breath to calm herself. This was no different than going on a mission, she had to control her pulse, control her mind, and think of the outcome.

The door opened. Uri was standing behind it a big smile on his face. He was wearing an Italian pinstriped dark grey suit, with a plum-colored shirt and deeply polished shoes. He looked every bit the successful businessman and yet if you looked a little closer you could see that there was a little bit of wear on the knees and elbows. The suit had been worn for many years, however, it still looked good on him.

"Miss Ramsey, it is so good to see you, ah, and your little dog. Please come in." He stepped back and opened the door into a large reception area. It was decorated much the same as the hallway and the walls were lined with pictures of his family. Straight in front of them, was a picture of Uri. It had pride of place and in it, he looked very regal.

"Thank you for seeing me so quickly. I really am a little stuck and any help you can give me would be a great assistance."

"Come on through and take a seat." He led her through into another room which had a beautiful view of the Bradford wharf or pool as some people called it. It was a man-made lake filled with boats of all kinds. Leading into it on the Lincoln side was the River Witham and going out of it was the Fossdyke Canal. Both were major waterways and got very busy.

"That's quite a view," Lola said and noticed the look of pride on his face. This man liked people to think he was influential, that he was rich, and that he was important. She could work with that.

Uri pointed to a black leather sofa which sat opposite to black leather chairs which surrounded an ornate coffee table that looked like it was made from an old root from some tree that had been polished and covered in glass. It was very beautiful.

"Can I offer you a drink?" Uri asked.

"Thank you, but I just had my lunch and I don't wish to impose."

Uri wandered over to a bar and poured himself two fingers of scotch. He swirled it around in his glass before returning to one of the chairs and sitting opposite her. After taking a small swig, he placed the glass on the glass table and then crossed his legs and folded his hands on top of them. "Tell me what you have?"

Lola had hoped he wouldn't ask this, for she had very little. However, she didn't have to tell the truth. Sassy pulled on her lead and Lola reached down and unclipped her. She sat there for a moment, feeling Uri's eyes on her, but as soon as he looked away she was gone. Lola hoped that she could find what they were looking for; what would happen then, she had no idea.

"I have been talking to a friend of a friend who has a man inside the Popov's business. They have been speaking about your brother, saying that something had to be done about him, but saying that it must not come back to them. I get the feeling they're scared of..." She had been about to say your father and realized that that was the wrong move. "Scared of you and your father. They don't want to upset you but they wanted your brother out of the way."

"This does not surprise me." Uri was shaking his head. "Maybe I should take it from here and give them Russian justice?"

"I don't know, I still haven't got substantiated proof that it was them. Perhaps you could help me find it?"

"I do not think so," he said and took another drink before banging the glass down on the coffee table a little bit harder.

What had she said to upset him? Or was this just an act? Lola knew she had to be careful, though she could look

ROSIE SAMS

after herself and she had Sassy, the last thing she wanted to do was get into an altercation with the Russian. She needed to find the evidence and get out. Once she had it, once she had something incontrovertible she could go to the police.

In her mind, she could hear Sassy moving about. The little dog often made grumbly mumbly sounds in her mind as she worked things out. "Oooh socks," Sassy said. This was what Lola had worried about. If he had a passport, and a spare passport, they could possibly be hidden in his wardrobe. The only problem was that would be somewhere close to his socks. Sassy had to keep her mind on the job but how could she tell her to do so?

"Wouldn't you rather see him rot in jail?" Lola asked.

"Not really, I think I've said enough. If you have someone who points to them then that is good enough for me. Where is your little dog?"

Oh dear, it looked like her ruse was over. "Oh, I'm sorry, she usually stays very close. I have panic attacks, she looks after me when they come on." Lola hadn't wanted to tell him it was PTSD. She did not wish to warn him that she was ex-military in case she had to protect herself in the future.

"Call her please, I don't wish her to leave any packages anywhere."

"I'm so sorry, of course. Sassy, come."

"Nearly got it," Sassy said. "Strong smell of passport thingy."

"I'm so sorry, perhaps I should go find her?" Lola asked.

"If Maxim and Ivan were out of the country, who do you think killed my brother?" Uri asked.

"I believe that they came back, I believe that they were only out of the country as an alibi," Lola said.

Uri's eyes narrowed. "I think you go now, with or without the little dog."

"I'm sorry, I'm sure your father would like you to help me," Lola said hoping that this would play to his vanity once more.

"Go, now. You are not fooling me!"

"Sassy, come, now," Lola said. This was what she had been afraid of. That Uri would realize that she did not think that the Popov's had used their trip abroad as an alibi, but that she thought he had.

"Was so close but can't find," Sassy said as she came trotting through with a pair of plum-colored socks in her mouth.

"What has she got?" Uri asked.

"I'm sorry, I should've expected this. She is rather obsessed with people's socks." Lola leaned down to Sassy and held her hand out. The little Frenchie turned her head with the socks in it away. Her ears were folded back and she was giving serious side-eye, she did not want to give up her prize.

"Give the socks to me," Lola said.

Sassy shook her head.

Lola wanted to tell her that this man was dangerous and that if she stole his socks he might even shoot them but, of course, she couldn't, he would think she was crazy. Lola looked back at Uri. His anger seemed to dissipate a little bit, perhaps he believed that Sassy was simply hunting for his socks.

"I'm so sorry," Lola said, "I will get them back for you."

"She can keep them but you must go, now!"

"Yes," Sassy said as she trotted to the elevator door with her prize held proudly before her.

FAILURE

*O*nce they were in the lift and on the way down Lola breathed a sigh of relief. There had been a moment or two there when she thought that Uri was on to them. When she thought that he wouldn't let them leave.

"Did you find any passports?" Lola asked.

"I find two, but I can't get to either," Sassy said. "One inside of a drawer, one in a shiny hard case, I can't open it. The laundry basket not far from there, and me found these great socks."

Lola chuckled, she thought that the socks had probably saved their lives. Uri couldn't imagine a little dog that would steal his socks would be any danger to him. Most people underestimated the little Frenchie. She was so small and so very very cute, and with a nose so short that no one believed she could find anything. That hubris of theirs was often their downfall. However, in this case, they had failed. They had found the evidence but had not been able to obtain it. What should they do now?

"Oh... I know now, that was the man who had been in the shed. He was the one I couldn't remember," Sassy said. "I sorry, I forgot."

"It's okay, you did really well," Lola said but she wished that they had found something they could take to the police, anything.

Outside the apartment block and along the waterfront there was a myriad of different cafés and eateries. Lola decided to have a coffee at one and to wait and see if Uri made a move.

She ordered coffee and a piece of cake and sat down to wait. Pulling out her phone she pretended she was reading something and angled herself so she could see the front of the apartment block.

"When we go home?" Sassy asked.

"When we have something," Lola said.

Sassy was looking up at Lola with that face that could melt the coldest heart and her little bottom lip was quivering. "You have cake, I have nothing."

"Oh, I'm sorry," Lola said and handed her down a small piece of cake.

"Me happy now."

Lola was happy too because Uri had just walked out of the building and headed across the front of the apartment block to a row of bins. He was carrying a black bag. As he got to the first bin he stopped and glanced around.

Lola kept herself behind her phone and hoped he would not see her. Quickly, she opened up the camera, went to video, and zoomed in. After glancing around and being sure he was not watched he ignored the first bin, and went down to the fourth. He opened it up, lifted out one of the bags, placed his bag inside, and then placed the other back on top of it. Dusting down his hands he glanced around once more before walking back to the building. Then he was gone.

Lola had filmed it all.

Maybe their failure was about to turn into success. Lola waited a full 10 minutes before she left the table and wandered over to the bins. No one else had been to them. She went to the fourth one, looked inside, pulled out the bag, and searched beneath it. The black bag that he had placed there was quite small, well, a large black bin bag but with very little in it. It was easy to find. When she felt it, she realized what it was. It was shredding. He had shredded his fake passport. Was this the end? Could the police put it back together?

"I smell passport," Sassy said.

"You are a clever girl."

*L*ola rang Wayne and told him what she had. "Should I come to the station? Should I take this to Daniel Peterson?"

"That is just amazing, but I am angry with you, Tanya would never forgive me if you were murdered by a Russian gangster!"

"I love you too," Lola said and chuckled.

"I think you should come in but I will talk to Chief Inspector Frances Weir, he will see to it that Daniel can't shove the evidence under the rug."

"The problem is," Lola said, feeling a little bit despondent, "the passport has been shredded. It's in long thin and I mean very thin strips. Will you be able to do anything with it? And will you be able to prove it's his?"

"I smelly it passport for you?" Sassy asked. "I smelly Uri all over it."

"Don't worry, the forensic team will be able to put it back together in next to no time. I'm pretty sure there will be plenty of DNA in there too. And fingerprints on the bag."

"You are just great, Wayne, thank you, we're on our way."

As Lola and Sassy made their way back to the car, Lola called Patricia and filled her in on what she had found. She agreed that she would be at the station as well and that she would keep an eye on things. She would make sure that the evidence was given the proper respect it deserved.

Lola was waiting at the station only three hours before the passport was put back together. She could hardly believe it, they had done a magnificent job and it was irrefutable evidence. Though Uri had tried to disguise his appearance by wearing a blond wig it was obvious that it was him. The bag also contained Eurostar tickets and car hire tickets. It appeared that he had hired a car and caught the train traveling back through the channel tunnel. They had him.

Lola and Patricia were drinking coffee in the corner of the precinct. They could see across the room into Chief Inspector Frances Weir's office. It looked like Daniel Peterson was getting a telling off. His head was bowed his hands held in front of him and he was nodding as the Chief Inspector spoke.

Peterson turned and left the room. His eyes glared at them for a moment and then he forced a smile on his face and walked across. "Miss Darnell, Miss Ramsey, I would like to thank you for the information that you have provided in this case. I will be preparing a team now to go to arrest Uri Petrov." Peterson was about to walk away.

"Wait just one moment," Patricia said. "When will you be releasing Father Jackson and Tony Munch?"

Peterson gulped and you could see his Adam's apple bouncing up and down his throat. "Detective Wayne Foster is already working on the paperwork. They will be out within the hour."

Peterson turned and left.

"I know they are out and they're free, but what about their reputations?" Lola asked Patricia.

"Don't worry, I have a friend at the local radio station. I will make sure that their innocence is blasted over the airways for the next 2 to 3 weeks. I will also get a big spread put in the local newspaper about this. I'm pretty sure Tony will get his job back if he wants it, and the same for Father Jackson. The church did not want to let him go, they felt they had to. I just wish people would wait for cases to be over rather than try people in the court of public opinion," Patricia said.

In front of them, Sassy was lying on the floor her legs out behind her, she was fast asleep.

"It looks like somebody's had a hard day," Patricia said.

"It's hard to explain, but I couldn't have found the evidence without her and I think she's exhausted. She will certainly be getting a few treats tonight."

Sassy's ears twitched at the word treat and she was instantly up and sitting in front of Lola. "I ready."

Once Uri Petrov had been brought into the station, Lola rang Borya and explained to him what had happened.

She could tell from the sadness in his voice that he had already known. After all, he had hinted to her who it was. For who else would he have not wanted to tackle? She felt sorry for him. To have lost one son, killed by the other, when you are dying yourself... it didn't bear thinking about.

"I'm so sorry about this," Lola said.

"Bud' Shto BUdyet, Whatever shall be, will be," he said. "I want to thank you for what you did for me and for coming back to me. I know not many people would be brave enough to ring me with such news. I am grateful for that. I know you did this for your friends but it means a lot that you told me yourself. I do not have long and I will be in the hospital from next week. If I ring you, would you bring your little dog to come to see me?"

"I would love to. Ring me anytime you want and we will be there."

FRIENDLY ADVICE

*I*t was three weeks after Father Jackson and Tony had been exonerated and life in the village was getting back to normal. Lola had only had a couple of easy cases and was enjoying the time off to relax and recuperate.

Tony and the father had insisted on paying her but she had given them only a small bill. It didn't seem fair to take money off them after all they had been through. However, they were still thanking her profusely every time she saw them.

Yesterday she had been to visit Borya in the hospital for the second time. He loved Sassy so much and she liked the old Russian too. This morning Lola had received a call to say that he had passed away but that he wanted to thank her and as such had left her a small sum in his will.

Lola was grateful but also felt a little awkward so she was walking to see Tilly. Somehow, she thought that her friend would be able to put this in perspective.

Sassy was pulling a little on her lead as she was so happy to be going to see Tilly.

"Wonder what treats Moley has for me?" Sassy asked.

"None if you call her that," Lola said.

Sassy spun around and sat in front of her, she tilted her head to the right. "Why, I mean nicely, she love me, I lovey her, I hungry."

"I'm sure she'll find something but it's not long since you had your breakfast." Luckily, Sassy kept trim, probably because of how active she was.

"I chase evil squirrels in garden, lots of running back and forth but they just disappear... and then reappear in trees."

Lola was not getting into that one. If she told Sassy that the squirrels could run straight up the trunk of a tree the little dog would be even more convinced that they were evil. Better to let her think they were just gone.

"We're here," Lola said and stepped into the shop.

Tilly was serving a customer but she waved and mouthed, just a minute. Lola wandered around the shop and picked up a few bits and pieces to take back to Tanya's. Once she had paid for them Tilly picked Sassy up and invited her into the back room. "Have I got something special for you," she said, whispering into Sassy's ear.

"Can't wait," Sassy said.

Once the tea was on Tilly brought out a tub from the fridge and took the lid off. "This is a new doggy recipe I tried. It is called Sardine Cake."

"Wow, it smells a bit strong," Lola said.

"Smells the best, fishy and delicious," Sassy said, sitting and looking up at Tilly with adoring eyes.

"I think she likes it," Lola said.

Tilly grinned and pointed at the pink fluffy bed she had bought for Sassy. The Frenchie spun in a circle and dived onto the bed, lying down instantly.

Tilly gave her a couple of bits of the Sardine Cake and they could both hear her grumbling and mumbling out her pleasure.

"How's your week been?" Tilly asked as she made the tea for them both.

"Good, I've just had a couple of jobs on."

Tilly served them both a cup of tea and sat down. "When are your renovations starting again?" she asked.

Lola sighed, builders had been working on her property restoring it, converting the downstairs into an office for her PI business and tidying up the upstairs for a living apartment. The bare bones of the building were in good order but it had been empty a long time and needed a bit of work. The problem was that Lola had used all her savings.

"I've run out of money again," Lola said, "So it will have to wait a little longer."

"What about your trust fund?" Tilly asked.

Lola felt her heart thump against her chest as a vision of her mother's angry face appeared before her. It was not the anger that cut her to the bone but the look of hurt in her mother's eyes. Lola shook her head. "I don't think I can use it, not for this."

Tilly reached out and took her hand. "I don't know what happened with your parents but if you ever want to talk

I'm here." Tilly waited but Lola shook her head. "Okay, I understand," she said. "However, I'm pretty sure that no matter what happened with your parents they would want you to be happy. They left you that money to help you, to support you, and to see that you had everything you needed."

"I know."

"But do you? You work hard but you seem to find it hard to take money off your clients. You must, you have to make a living or you will no longer be able to help them. Use your trust fund, your parents would want you to."

Lola nodded, she knew that Tilly was right but she also knew that she had to read the letter first, the one her parents left her. For some reason, she wasn't ready to read it yet. In her mind, they said they understood that they loved her and were happy for her, if they didn't, if in the letter they still blamed her, she was afraid it would set her PTSD back and that she would be having nightmares and panic attacks again on a daily basis.

"I will think about it," Lola said.

"I guess that's a start." Tilly smiled but the bell to her shop ended their conversation.

"I should be going, thanks," Lola said and followed Tilly back to the shop where Lucinda Clifton-West had just come in.

The woman was in her seventies, around 5 foot 4, and rather plump with a large nose and round cheeks. Her messy blonde hair sat atop beady brown eyes and in her hands was a pile of flyers. "Morning Tilly, I want to put a few of these posters up in the shop. It's a safety issue, for the good of the village."

"Oh, really," Tilly said, "Let me see."

Lucinda handed over a poster and Lola saw what it said. Oh dear, this was not good.

> Cut back the hedges.
> Keep our village safe.
> People before Yew.

"I'm sorry, Lucinda, but I can't agree with you," Tilly said and handed back the poster.

"Really! Do you think hedges are worth more than people?"

"No, of course not, I just don't think the hedges have to be cut to save people, good day."

Lucinda stood there for a moment looking from Lola to Tilly and back again When she got no support, she turned on her heels and was gone.

"Oh, before you go, I do have a flyer for you," Tilly said with a grin and reached under the counter and handed one over.

Welcome Home Garden Party

3rd May 11am behind the Church

Guests of Honor:

Tony Munch

Father Jackson

Lola Ramsay

Sassy

Lola smiled, Father Jackson and Tony had already told her and she was already embarrassed, after all, she had just been doing her job.

"Tony told me you weren't going." Tilly shook her head. "I won't have it, you have to be there."

"Okay," Lola said. The party was just three weeks away and she hoped that they would have forgotten by then, but somehow she doubted it.

OH OH

*L*ola and Sassy were getting ready to go to the Welcome Home Party. It had been a busy few weeks since Tony and Father Jackson were cleared.

Lola had been called to the offices of Borya Financials. At first, she had worried about going, what could they want? However, in his will, Borya had left her 3 million pounds. Lola had tried to turn it down but was told she couldn't.

Tilly had sat her down and told her she must use some to continue with the renovations to her property. Lola had reluctantly agreed and the work was back on track. Tilly then asked her why she was so afraid of money.

Lola had never thought about it that way but she realized that she did feel uneasy about it. After some long thought she couldn't work out the reasons and the money was still eating away at her. They were nearly ready to go but she was sitting on the bed staring into the past, still in her dog-walking trousers that were a little muddy from their morning walk.

Sassy looked up at her. "Sad?"

"Not really."

"You are, tell me." Sassy pawed her leg and gave her little Frenchie grin.

"I have been given some money and I feel wrong using it."

Sassy tilted her head and then shook it. "No understand, what is money?"

"You've seen those notes I give to people when I buy things, that is money."

"That silly, what use are they?" Sassy stared up at her, her eyes wide as she tried to work out what the problem was. "Maybe they good to shake and tear up." Sassy growled and mimicked killing a toy.

"I can swap the notes for toys and treats, money is useful."

"Then that good, why make you sad? If Tyson gives me bally, I happy." Certain she had solved the problem Sassy jumped up onto the bed and crawled onto Lola's lap. "Cuddles always help."

Lola kissed her between the ears. "Yes, they do, come on, let's go."

Lola got up thinking over the last few weeks and how things were going. It was all good. She had solved a few cases and all of them had been easy, either background checks, one missing person who had turned up at a friend's house asleep and hungover, and one divorce case.

Wayne and Tanya had already left for the garden party that was being held behind the church and had made Lola promise that she would follow them. Though she didn't want to go she knew she had to. They would come looking for her if she didn't.

"Can I wear tiara?" Sassy asked, "I want to be a princess."

"Of course," Lola said as she pulled on a clean pair of trousers. She was wearing a plum-colored blouse and now black trousers. She looked okay. Running a comb through her hair she fastened it back and applied a touch of makeup. "Will I do?"

"Yes," Sassy said. "Go, me need cake."

As they walked past Roy Patterdale's Lola let out a groan. In 4 places the hedge had been massacred. It had been cut so far back that you could see right through to the middle. It was all bare branches that looked as if they were dead. Oh no, what would Roy do? The devastation looked so awful against the rest of the pristine hedge. Roy must be livid.

Lola walked through the churchyard and around to the garden where the party was in full swing. There were trestle tables set out with food on them and another table with cocktails. The scent of hot dogs, burgers, and chicken drifted over from the grill, the barbeque as it was called here. Tony was manning it in a blue striped apron. The sun was shining and everyone seemed to be having a great time.

"Ah, here she is," Father Jackson shouted as Lola walked in.

Oh no, she didn't want this but Tony had handed his tongs to another man and came up to her with Tyson.

"Thanks for helping Tony man," Tyson said.

Lola stroked the boxer's soft head, he thanked her every time.

"I can't thank you enough," Tony said. "I really can't."

"You don't need to thank me." Lola was led up to the front where the father told the whole village what had happened. They were clapping and Lola knew that her cheeks were beetroot red.

Once the ordeal was over she made her way across to Tilly, Wayne, Tanya, and Alice. As always, Alice was wearing a shell suit, this one was pink, purple, and white. It was very bright but not as bright as Alice's smile as she waved Lola over.

"Morning," Alice said, "We are all so proud of you." She pulled Lola into a hug.

"Join us for a cocktail," Tanya said winking as she knew how much Lola hated the fuss.

"I think I need it," Lola said.

Sassy and Tyson were wandering around but close by. They were picking up any bit of dropped food. Lola could hear Sassy explain to Tyson how to do it. The boxer was a little nervous. He didn't like being this close to people.

"Try this," Sassy said. She walked up to a couple with plates in their hands and sat in front of them. Then she stood on her back legs and waved her front paws. They laughed and tossed her a bit of sausage.

"Wow, that is magic," Tyson said. "I could never do that."

"I will teach you."

Lola pulled her focus away from the dogs, they were fine and all the village knew them. Sassy would not go far. In front of her, she noticed that Lucinda Clinton-West was smirking at Roy. Roy's face was red, his fists clenched. Lola started to move but Father Jackson beat her to it.

"Come on you two, no hostility, not today." The father took them both to the table. "Shake hands and toast with a cocktail. Here, a Mai Tie will make you both feel better."

Roy didn't move. "Trust me," the father said, "Life is too short."

"My hedge is too short," Roy barked.

"Now, now, not today, have a drink for me."

Roy didn't move for a moment but Father Jackson kept his eyes on him. Roy squirmed under that stern gaze and eventually nodded. Roy sighed and reached out his hand. Lucinda took it but the smile on her face was awfully smug as she shook.

"Now, get a drink, both of you," Father Jackson said.

Roy picked up two of the orange cocktails and handed one to Lucinda.

She smiled and took a drink. Roy walked away with his and Lola watched as he threw it away.

"Maybe I should go talk to him," Lola said.

"No, leave him for now," Tilly said. "He needs time to calm down."

"I'm not sure he will ever calm down, the hedge looks awful and he has put in so much work to keep it so nice. So many years of effort have been destroyed," Lola said.

"Life in a small village." Wayne laughed. "I used to think it was quiet and peaceful. London was easier!"

Tanya playfully thumped his shoulder. "You love it here, really."

He shook his head as if to disagree and then laughed. "Okay, I do, but only because you are here." With that, he kissed Tanya.

"Hark at these two," Alice said, "Young love's a grand thing."

They moved forward in the line and Lola felt Sassy touch her leg. "Lady not well," she said.

"What?" Lola asked.

"What what?" Tanya asked.

"Sorry I was talking to myself," Lola said blushing.

At that moment they all turned as Lucinda made a horrid retching sound and threw up her Mai Tai before collapsing onto the grass.

"Oh oh," Sassy said. "Told you, lady not well."

Read on for 2 Recipes...

If you enjoyed this book grab Mai Ties and Murder now.

The Art of Murder

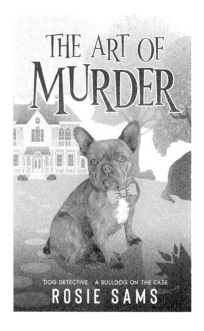

The Case of the Mix-Up Murder

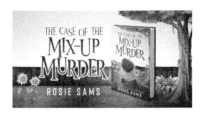

The Bulldog and the Buried Body

To be the first to find out when Rosie releases a new book and to hear about other sweet romance authors join the exclusive SweetBookHub readers club here.

If you enjoyed this book, Rosie and Lila would appreciate it if you left a review on Amazon or Goodreads.

RASPBERRY IRISH CREAM TIRAMISU

INGREDIENTS

For the fruit

- 500g of frozen raspberries – you can use fresh but frozen gives more moisture
- 50g of caster sugar
- 1 heaped tbsp of cornflour

For the Tiramisu

- 250g of mascarpone cheese
- 600ml of double cream
- 6 tbsp icing sugar
- 1 tbsp vanilla extract
- 450m of oz strong coffee

- 40ml Irish Cream Liqueur
- 12 trifle sponges, halved through the middle to make 24
- 100g of plain chocolate

Method For the Fruit:

1. Heat the frozen berries with the caster sugar in a saucepan over a medium heat, stirring, until all the sugar has dissolved and the berries have just defrosted.
2. Sieve the fruit over a bowl separating out the whole, unpressed fruit with the liquid.
3. Pour the fruit liquid back into the saucepan.
4. Mix the cornflour with 2 tablespoons of cold water in a bowl until smooth.
5. Add to the pan and mix together.
6. Stir over a medium heat until boiling and allow to thicken. The sauce should coat the back of a spoon.
7. Add the whole fruit back to the saucepan, mix gently.
8. Set aside to cool completely.

Method For the Tiramisu:

1. Add the mascarpone, cream, sugar and vanilla into a large bowl.
2. Whisk together to form light, soft peaks – being careful not to over-whisk.
3. Mix the coffee and Irish Cream together.
4. Soak half of the sponges in the coffee and Irish cream mixture.
5. Arrange the soaked sponges over the base of your trifle dish dish.
6. Spread a third of the cream mixture on top and grate on half the chocolate.
7. Spoon all the raspberries on top in an even layer.
8. Soak the remaining sponges in coffee and Irish Cream and arrange on top in another layer.
9. Spread half of the cream on top and grate over the remaining chocolate.
10. Pipe the remaining cream around the edge of the dish.
11. Chill for 1–2 hours.
12. Enjoy.

SARDINE CAKE FOR DOGS

Ingredients:

2 x 120 g tins of sardines in tomato sauce

300 g flour (can use rice flour or ground oats)

2 eggs

50 g strong cheddar

1 tablespoon oil

Method:

1. Crack the eggs into a large measuring bowl. Grate the cheese, and add to the eggs along with the tins of sardines. Blend with a fork.
2. Mix in the flour until a nice firm consistency. Add more flour if needed.
3. Pour contents into a greased loaf tin, sprinkle the grease with flour to prevent sticking and spread evenly.
4. Bake at 180 degrees for 25-30 minutes, until springy when pressed. A knife should come out clean.
5. Allow to cool before removing from the tin.
6. Divide into portions, use or freeze.

* * *

Rosie is a member of SweetBookHub.com, a place where you can find
amazing fun books that are sweet and suitable for all ages. Join the
exclusive newsletter and get 3 free books here

Printed in Great Britain
by Amazon

80051579R00188